DORN

After the Civil War ended, Bat Dorn had nothing to go home to — until he got a letter from his buddy Sarge Hoak inviting him to join him in Warbonnet. Sarge already owned the general store; he told Dorn if they opened a saloon they could make a killing in that town.

Things did not turn out to be quite that simple . . .

DORN

G. G. Boyer

GUNSMOKE

This hardback edition 2002
by Chivers Press
by arrangement with
Golden West Literary Agency

ISBN 0 7540 8189 3

British Library Cataloguing in Publication Data available.

Printed and bound in Great Britain by
BOOKCRAFT, Midsomer Norton, Somerset

CHAPTER 1

THE horse was dead for sure. It hadn't looked like much of a horse. But it'd had enough heart to save Dorn's life before it died. He looked regretfully at its inert form. Maybe if he hadn't had to make it run, it would have survived. He cautiously crept up to the crest of the hill, peeking over at their back trail through the tangled branches of a sage. The Indians were still there, about a mile away. They likely wouldn't follow under the circumstances. In the first place they didn't know he was unarmed. In the second, his dead horse was out of their sight so they might think he was already far away. Besides they were not likely to abandon the slaughtered beef he'd stumbled onto them butchering—the reason they'd shot at him.

"Friendlies!" Dorn snorted under his breath. He felt anger rising in him now over the fate they'd dealt his faithful old flea-bitten nag. Maybe if it had looked like more of a horse he'd have felt less pity for it. It hadn't even been his. He'd more or less borrowed it.

Peering intently toward the redskins he said to himself, "Only two. Well, old hoss, I'll get even with those bastards for you if it's the last thing I do."

The trouble had started as Dorn was riding along, half asleep. He'd nursed a pint of whiskey for twenty-five miles and tossed the bottle away. The night before he'd been plucked clean in a poker game. He'd salvaged just enough to buy that pint. They'd got his Twenty-fifth Infantry mustering-out pay and his six-shooter. Also the gold watch he'd taken off the body of a Union colonel when he'd ridden with Mosby in the war. It had been his good-luck piece. He'd

5

often hocked it but never sacrificed it before. And finally he'd lost the gold cuff links that had belonged to his father. He'd always hoped the old man hadn't missed them too badly since. At the time there hadn't been a clean white shirt in Northern Virginia. They had been the only memento he'd carried from his old Virginia home when he'd ruefully surrendered the second time. That time he'd been whipped by trying to grow cotton, corn, and sweet taters. It wasn't his style. Besides Reconstruction had graveled him. That had been ten years before, in 1868. The cuff links, too, had often been hocked.

He'd spent the intervening decade in the damn-Yankee army. It beat starving. Besides, the cards usually had a way of substantially supplementing his thirteen dollars a month—such as by a multiple of ten or so. It hadn't been a bad life. But the old pasteboards had finally done him in for sure the night before. Likely he'd had a little too much to drink. On top of that, the other players weren't a bunch of army recruits—they'd been pros. So—cleaned, without a friend in town, he'd set off to hoof it the seventy-five miles to Warbonnet. A damn-fool stunt, some would have called it, especially without a gun. But pilgrims had made it across the Oregon Trail on foot without a gun. And Old Sarge Hoak's letter had been a great incentive. Dorn had missed Sarge. It hadn't been too bad when Sarge first took his discharge, because he'd stayed around as post sutler. But then they'd caught President Grant's crony, General Belknap, and found out how a lot of guys like Sarge had bought sutlerships. So Hoak had moved over to Warbonnet and started a general store.

His letter had said: "I got a good deal over here. If you come over we can start a saloon too. We'll get the big eaters in the store and the big drinkers in the saloon. Besides I got a good deal going with the Indian Agent over at Ft. Littleworth reservation. I'll tell you about it when you get here. We're both bound to get well."

It had sounded good to Dorn. He'd just stopped for a

breather and reread Sarge's letter, then stuffed it back in his pocket beside his pint, when he'd first spotted the pinto crowbait. It hadn't even run when he approached it. Instead it had looked at him, then walked right up to him. "Maybe some kid's pet," he'd told himself. "I shouldn't borrow it." He'd looked around warily for a homesteader's cabin anywhere in view. There was nothing but bare prairie and the empty road stretching both ways to the horizon. He'd patted the horse's nose and scratched its ears. Cautiously he'd grasped its mane at the withers and swung himself onto it, bareback. He'd found that someone savvy had trained it to respond to leg pressure, so it was no problem to get it started down the road. About a mile along he'd found a length of rope, probably dropped by a freighter, and got off to fashion a hackamore.

Now Dorn sadly looked at the faithful, trusting, dead animal. "I bet you was quite a hoss in your day," he said to it. "And you was quite a hoss today." He uttered a silent prayer for his savior, then returned to watch the Indians.

By then they'd got most of the beef and its hide on a travois. He watched them move off. After what he considered a safe interval he started a long circuit to intercept their trail, armed only with his hackamore rope and a barlow pocketknife. At least the travois marks wouldn't be hard to follow. He wondered at those Indians' gall, first taking a shot at him, probably because they'd taken him for a cowboy, then moving off slowly and leaving a plain trail. They had to be fairly desperate for something to eat, he reasoned.

Dorn figured he had seven or eight hours of daylight left for trailing. He set off at the determined swinging pace of a professional infantryman. A good doughboy could outwalk the cavalry. He and a thousand others had often proven it, as on Crook's Starvation March a couple of years before, which Dorn had accompanied all the way, ending up fitter than when he'd started.

He'd been shot at today where the country had first risen

to foothills, with the higher snow-capped peaks showing clearly on the horizon. The Indian trail led through a steep-walled canyon of red rock, which Dorn skirted by a tortuous couple-of-mile detour over some wicked boulder-strewn ridges. Topping out, he spotted his quarry far ahead, moving northward up a broad park which rose toward the first timber. Good, he thought. I can parallel them at least as far as the timber, then cut their trail again. He struck out through the brushy ground at the valley's edge where he wouldn't be easily spotted. Once well camouflaged in the brush he broke into a dogtrot. As the Department of the Platte's heavyweight boxing champion he'd kept his legs in extra good shape by running year round. He knew he could jog all day at his present pace, uphill or down.

The sun was already behind the mountain peaks when he overtook the two braves. He might have stumbled directly onto them except that they were making absolutely no attempt to conceal their presence. They had a smoky fire going. It was only two years since Custer's fiasco at the Little Big Horn, so Dorn suspected the few pioneer cattlemen in this country still had a thoroughgoing respect for Poor Lo. The conduct of these two Indians revealed that they were aware of this. They expected no one to have the guts to follow them.

Dorn circled around to the far side of their camp. Probably got squaws here, he reasoned. I hope they don't have any damn dogs. He was consoled by the speculation that, hungry as they seemed to be, they'd probably eaten all their dogs. Before it got full dark he was able to spot a single tepee through the trees. He carefully stalked the camp, slipping close enough to see two braves and two squaws by the fire. They were all young—little more than kids in his judgment. So much the better, he thought. Easier to take. The smell of roasting beef tantalized him. He'd thought his best time to surprise them would be morning, but his stomach changed his mind. Besides, by morning his stomach might be growling loud enough to give him away.

He had carefully observed where the rifles of the two braves were leaning against two trees. He'd also noted they were both good repeating Winchesters. This called up the rueful thought of the army's crummy single-shot Springfields with their defective ammunition, not the least of the causes of Custer's disaster. He dearly wanted to get his hands on one of those Winchesters, undetected. However, he didn't wish to kill any of these people; in fact, in his heart he felt genuine sympathy for all these tribes whose way of life so sadly was dying. Besides, he knew there was nothing personal about the shot that had killed his horse. The Indians were hungry, perhaps starving. An empty stomach made a man desperate, as the smell of their beef reminded him again.

He worked up directly behind the tree supporting the closest Winchester, hoping the sound of their talk and laughter would cover any sound he inadvertently made. He planned to grab one Winchester, work the lever to get their attention, and cover them while he got the other rifle. After that he'd play it by ear, depending on their reaction. He was confident he could easily kill them all if he had to. He might have to. Squaws were no mean fighters either. They'd killed many a chivalrous army dummy while he'd hesitated to shoot a woman.

His plan went off perfectly up to a point. He easily grabbed the Winchester and levered the action noisily open and shut. He'd planned to catch the ejected cartridge and put it back in the magazine later. Only there was no ejected shell. The gun was empty. He disgustedly regarded the four Indians who had all leaped to their feet, then paused, ready to attack. Hastily he grabbed the other Winchester.

One of the braves laughed. "Empty too," he said in good English. "You look."

Then all the Indians laughed, spreading out to circle him with drawn knives, the squaws too. In desperation he scooped up an egg-sized rock and with the skill acquired as the star pitcher of the Twenty-fifth Infantry nine, knocked one of the braves out cold with a perfect strike between his eyes. This drastically changed the odds. The other three, shaken by this demonstration, froze. The brave who'd first spoken in English resheathed his knife, then smiled.

"You want some chuck?" he asked, pointing at the beef.

"Sure," Dorn said.

The Indian approached him, hand advanced to shake in the style of the whites. Dorn was ready for the slightest sign of treachery. And it came. The brave started a lightning move for his knife. Ready for this, Dorn delivered the old one-two—a solid left to the gut, followed by a right cross to the jaw. The brave quietly collapsed and joined his buddy among the twittering birdies.

Keeping a close eye on the two squaws, Dorn used his hackamore rope to truss up the two braves, back to back. Then by signs he told the two women to toss their knives on the ground and step away from them.

"Plenty strong," one of the squaws said to the other in English, pointing at him.

By then he was putting away generous slices of their beef, sawed off with one of their own knives.

"Help yourselves," he invited them tossing back one knife.

They'd been secretly conferring, giggling occasionally and pointing both at him and at their unconscious menfolk.

"Hokay," said the one who'd spoken a little English. She took the knife and cut herself and the other a big hunk of roast beef.

"We go with you," she said around a mouthful of beef. "You big chief." Pointing at the two braves she said disgustedly, "Little boys."

Dorn laughed. He didn't know whether they'd understand him or not, but he said, "That's the best offer I've had today, ladies. I'll think about it."

"Hokay," the squaw said again, and nodded. He still wasn't sure she understood much English or really knew what he'd said. But she looked happy, putting herself around some more beef.

Well, he consoled himself, I got even for the old hoss so far. Maybe even got myself an outfit. He had to admit both young squaws were pretty as new harmonicas. He wondered what Old Sarge would say if he showed up with a tepee, two squaws, and a remuda of Injun ponies.

Just then a motion and noise at the edge of the firelight caused him to explode into a long dive and somersault away from the light. He crawled to his feet and sprung toward the deeper darkness before he turned to face his new threat. He had trouble believing what greeted his gaze.

"I'll be go-to-hell!" he exclaimed.

His supposedly dead pinto crowbait entered the circle of firelight and paused, looking around for him. The bullet hole was still in its chest, surrounded by clotted blood. Dorn reentered the circle of firelight first—the squaws had also taken to their heels.

"Okay, ladies," he called. "Safe to come back."

He was exploring the bullet hole with his finger. The big lead slug was just under the skin. He worked it out; the Indians' last bullet, apparently.

"A short round," he muttered to himself. "Old Paint here musta keeled over from too much exertion. Poor old guy probably has a bad ticker."

It was the first time he'd known horses fainted.

Old Paint was nuzzling him affectionately.

"Don't that beat a hog flying?" Dorn asked himself.

The next morning he started the two braves on foot down their trail to the Fort Littleworth reservation with a swift kick apiece in the breechcloth.

"An' keep goin'," he cautioned them. They did. They'd had enough of his medicine.

The two squaws happily broke camp for him, and the three of them set off. When they got to Warbonnet, he had the squaws set up the tepee along the Rosebloom River near the edge of town. Then he mounted the best of his recently acquired string of ponies, using a gaudy Indian blanket for a saddle, and set off to find Sarge Hoak.

CHAPTER 2

WARBONNET gained birth when Fort Littleworth was established as one of several posts in the hostile Indian country, following the Custer disaster. It was a trifle over a year old when Dorn first saw it. Mostly it was two parallel wide, dusty streets, when they weren't muddy, running perpendicular to the Rosebloom. An alley separated them. At the river the army had jerrybuilt a strange pole bridge on the road to the fort, which was four miles west.

Dorn had no trouble finding the old sarge. The largest building on the four-block-long street, two stories high with an ornate false-fronted third story, bore a massive hanging sign protruding across the boardwalk, proclaiming Hoak's Mercantile. Dorn tied his pony at the hitch rail, mounted the two steps to the walk, and went inside. Sarge was standing at the top of a ladder which ran along the tiered shelves on a track, reaching down a bolt of cloth for a little old lady. He trundled it down and rolled off a sample on the counter.

"With you in a minute," he said to Dorn, not looking at him.

"That's okay," Dorn said. "I'd rather see you alone—I got some more rustled beef."

The lady turned to glare at Dorn, mouth open, then back to Sarge, who looked startled, then irritated. Then, recognizing Dorn, he broke into a grin from ear to ear. The lady looked at Sarge as though he might be going a trifle tetched, grinning after what had just been said.

"Never mind, Mrs. Perkins," Sarge said. "This lunatic is an old friend pullin' my leg. He's too shiftless to rustle cattle."

Mrs. Perkins still looked severe and unsettled. Finally,

after a reproachful look at them both over her glasses, she grinned. "Oh, I see," she said. "He's being funny?"

"Trying to be," Sarge said. To Dorn he suggested, "Go back and raid the crackers and cheese or something till I take care of Mrs. Perkins."

Dorn took him up on that. He noticed that Sarge showed the results of prosperity. His good-natured jowly face was porkier, and an extra fifteen pounds of happy dinners, or beer, or both, hung over his pants waist. He was the picture of a typical bartender rather than a storekeeper, black oily hair, even a spit curl, shiny protruding blue eyes, and all. Dorn had noticed when Sarge was on the ladder that he still moved his bearish six-foot frame around nimbly enough, however. Probably still got a punch like getting kicked by a horse, Dorn thought.

When the customer was gone, Sarge came back to where Dorn sat on the counter, feet dangling, munching crackers and cheese, chased with a ginger beer.

"Got the real thing on ice out back," Sarge said. "How about it?"

"Why not?"

In the storage room a clerk was opening boxes of canned goods.

"How about takin' over out front, Ikey," Sarge said. "Meet my old sidekick, Dorn," he added. The two shook hands and Ikey disappeared out front.

Sarge retrieved two cold beers out of the ice room and opened them, handing one to Dorn. He hooked a stool over toward him with his toe and flopped himself into a swivel chair at his rolltop desk. This section was obviously his office.

"Ahhh!" Sarge exhaled luxuriantly after his first big swig of cold beer. Dorn imitated him. Sarge said, "I've had a beer on my mind all day. Been busy till now. Business falls off this time of the afternoon." He took another big, gurgling swig. "So tell your old Sarge what's been happenin' to you since I saw you."

Dorn told him about the last couple of days. He finished with the announcement that he had two young squaws in a tepee down by the river.

"That's rich," Sarge guffawed. "Leave it to you. Ever' time I turned my back you had another dame hangin' around your neck. Maybe I'd better go down with you and glim these two if they're lookers like you say."

"Later," Dorn suggested. "Besides I'm married to both of 'em just now."

"Married! Who the hell married you?" Sarge snorted, grinning.

"God," Dorn assured him. "Or Wakan Tanka, maybe. All proper in the eyes of the Almighty whatever."

"Balls," Sarge said. "You ain't the marryin' kind."

They were interrupted by gunfire somewhere down the alley a block or more. Sarge moved to the door and peeked out into the alley. Dorn followed cautiously, very much aware that he was still unarmed.

"It's that drunk son-of-a-bitch, Cantoon, again," Sarge said. "Him and some of his boys."

Dorn looked out in time to see a figure scamper for cover ahead of a pair of bullets that kicked up the dust behind his heels. Sarge grumbled, "That was my damn marshal that just headed for his hole."

Dorn didn't miss that. "Waddya mean *your* marshal?"

"I'm mayor," Sarge told him, then ignoring Dorn's gleeful snort, added, "Let's go out front for some artillery and take a hand in this game." That forestalled an inquiry into how he'd garnered that exalted office.

He led the way back into the front of the store to the gun case, picked himself a double-barreled shotgun, and handed Dorn a six-shooter and box of shells. Sarge slipped a couple of buckshot loads into his shotgun, sliding a half-dozen extra shells into his pocket.

"I don't want him hurt too fatal unless we have to," Sarge said. "He's my cheap beef supplier, if you know what I mean."

Dorn did. When he'd made his earlier remark to Sarge about rustled stock he'd known there was an eight-to-five chance he'd hit an exposed nerve.

"He's drunk, naturally," Sarge observed.

"How d'ya know?" Dorn asked.

"He's always drunk," Sarge said. "I'll try to get him to come down here and we'll reason with him with this shotgun."

There was more yelling and shooting, this time closer.

"Here he comes," Sarge said. He stepped out with the shotgun leveled. "Hey, Cantoon," he bellered.

Dorn stepped out behind Sarge with his pistol shoved in his waistband.

Cantoon spurred his horse and came thundering at them waving his pistol. As he passed he fired a shot in the air, drunk, but nonetheless mindful of that scattergun pointed at him. He whirled his mount and started to thunder by again, his head level with the waists of the two men on the store's rear loading platform. Dorn had stepped behind a pickle barrel for shelter in case Cantoon aimed his way. As the drunken rider passed him he neatly picked him off his horse with a singletree someone had thoughtfully leaned against the barrel. It made a sort of interesting plunk as it contacted the cowboy's hat. Cantoon sprawled off into a fresh pile of horse manure.

"Hey," one of Cantoon's cronies yelled. "That jasper just clouted the boss."

There were three others, and they gathered as though for a concerted charge. Then they remembered Sarge and his scattergun.

"Why don't you boys go up to the Troopers' Delight and have a couple on me," Sarge yelled.

One of the three cocked his hat back with his pistol barrel and scratched his head with the front sight. "Damn if that don't sound like a helluva good idea. Let's go, boys." He spurred his horse and accidentally shot his own hat off as the horse suddenly leaped into motion. He looked reproachfully at his smoking pistol as he galloped away, the rest following.

His punctured hat remained in the alley where it had fallen.

"Well," Sarge said. "Let's get a bucket of water and slosh it on old Cantoon there."

The cowboy leader's horse was idly cropping the grass growing in patches along the store's rear.

It took two buckets of water to get a twitch out of Cantoon. First he put his hands experimentally to his head. Then he groaned.

"What hit me?" he asked groggily. His eyes were beginning to focus.

Sarge pointed a thumb at Dorn. "He hit you," he said.

Cantoon glared at Dorn. "I'll git you fer that, pilgrim," he growled.

"I wouldn't try that if I was you," Sarge advised him.

Cantoon glared at Sarge. "Why not? Who the hell does he think he is?"

Sarge looked slyly. "Most likely you ain't heard of him up here. That's Bat Dorn. Even old Wild Bill walked wide around him when we was all after the Comanches down south."

"Bat Dorn?" Cantoon mouthed the name. It had a nice sound to it. He was convincing himself he must have heard of someone so "pizen" Wild Bill avoided him.

He looked at Dorn with a new respect in his eyes. "Hell." He excused himself. "We was jist lettin' off a little steam. What brings you up here, Mr. Dorn?"

Sarge hastily said, "He's our new marshal. And you can call him Bat—he ain't proud."

They hauled Cantoon to his feet and sent him staggering on down to the Troopers' Delight to get some medicine for his bump. Then Sarge elbowed Dorn and chuckled with satisfaction. "Right now I'll bet he's telling the boys he seen Bat Dorn hisself from only that far away. Won't do your reputation no harm, Bat."

"Hell, I ain't no gunman," Dorn protested. "You'll get me killed, tellin' people such lies."

"Naw, I won't," Sarge countered. "By the time I get through talking you up, there won't be anyone dare touch a gun around you. C'mon inside. I got something you can use. A Texas quick-draw scabbard. It's all carved too."

"Where'd you get one of them?" Dorn asked.

"A guy left it with me."

"What makes you so sure he won't come back for it?"

"He's up in Boot Hill."

Dorn gave him a long look. "Where I'll probably be if I go to actin' like a gunman."

"No sweat," Sarge said. "Just let the old Sarge here handle advertising your rep."

He tossed Dorn the rig.

"Hey," Dorn said. "This thing is for a lefty."

"I know," Sarge said. "It'll give you an advantage. Wear a coat and keep your business gun out of sight in your right back pocket."

"I thought you wanted me to run a saloon and gambling layout?" Dorn protested.

Sarge eyed him in disgust. "Did you ever know a marshal that didn't run a saloon and gambling joint? And provide a few willing ladies on the side, too, for that matter. I can see it now. We'll call it Bat's Place. It's a natural, you bein' famous and all. C'mon Bat. I'll take you down to the Troopers' Delight to meet the boys."

Dorn followed reluctantly, shaking his head.

"Bat," he mumbled disgustedly under his breath. "Bat Dorn." He had to admit he sort of liked the catchy sound of it himself—and the way the saloon quieted down when he walked in.

CHAPTER 3

DORN had a flash of insight about how to handle himself as a man with a big reputation. He'd had a season watching the best of them, Wild Bill Hickok, when he was sheriff at Hays City. Recalling Hickok's manner, Dorn paused inside the doors, coldly looked the house over, very poker-faced, then silently headed for the end of the bar where he took up a position, back to the wall. He nodded once at the crowd. Sarge took a place beside him. Conversation resumed in a lower key. Dorn speculated from the looks in his direction that most of it was about him. Sarge won his bet that Cantoon would soon bring his crew over and gain a little reflected glory by introducing them to the man who'd flattened him with a singletree.

Sarge introduced him to some of the "bhoys" from the fort, in for a payday toot with a few of their sergeants. He was glad to see that none of them was anyone he knew that might give him away. He'd started to enjoy his new role. In the back of his mind, however, was an unhappy little reservation that had to do with how well he'd like it if he really had to live up to his newfound reputation. He didn't have long to live in comparative peace with that nagging question.

"Yahoo!" someone yelled on the boardwalk out front. Obviously the same someone almost knocked off the batwing doors as he charged inside and again yelled, "Yahoo!"

Sarge said quickly in a low voice, "That's Yahoo Dave Storms. Thinks he's the granddaddy bare-knuckle champ in the territory. Got a glass jaw under that bush he wears. I whipped his butt myself one night over at the store. He's a freighter. Hates all sojer boys."

18

As many eyes were turned on Dorn as on Yahoo Dave, wondering what move he might make. He simply looked Dave's way once, then asked Sarge, "Is he a shootist?"

"Naw. Strictly fists. Or a club if he needs one maybe."

Dave obviously had quite a load on already. He swayed on his feet, glaring at the troops, all of whom had at least heard of him. "Got m' boys outside," he stated. "Bringin' 'em in fer a drink. Any o' you tin sojers got any perticker objections?"

If they hadn't up till then, he was perfectly aware they now did. Besides it was a familiar challenge. Hallenbeck's Glassware of Chicago regularly supplied the Troopers' Delight with about a hundred dollars' worth of new glasses every month.

Sarge nudged Dorn. "It's now or never, if you're gonna be Bat Dorn. Otherwise you'll have to take them two squaws somewhere else."

Feeling more like a goat than a Bat, Dorn took a deep breath and crossed the room to confront Yahoo Dave. The room grew at least quiet enough to hear a poker chip drop. Even Dave sensed the new element and tried to focus his eyes on the rapidly approaching marshal. Before he could open his yawp again, Marshal Bat Dorn made his first official move. He knocked Dave out cold with one roundhouse right to the jaw. Then he stepped out onto the walk where he'd seen some of Dave's compadres gawking over the batwings, waiting for their cue to storm inside.

"I'm the new marshal. Anybody else care for a waltz?"

A freighter half a head taller than Yahoo Dave stepped forward. Dorn didn't even give him time to open his mouth. He delivered the one-two that had dropped the Indian brave the previous night.

"Now," he said, in a tone that indicated he had them surrounded and would graciously accept their surrender when he pleased, "We got a new set of rules around here. You want to break up a saloon, see me first. I'm sellin' permits at five dollars a damn fool to cover the busted stuff and doctor's bill. You want to come in and mix it up, shuck out at the door. I'll be in to join you. I'd rather fight than eat any day."

Dorn knew that everyone inside could clearly hear him. "That goes for you troopers, too," he said, raising his voice a little. Knowing from the look of the crowd of freighters that he'd get no takers, he ordered, "A couple of you boys come in an' drag Yahoo Dave out. And tell him what I said when he comes to. Now why don't you pick a saloon where the troopers don't hang out—unless you get that permit."

He turned on his heel and returned to his position at the end of the bar. Sarge said in a loud voice, "In case any o' you birds wondered why they call him Bat, now you know. He's twice that good with a six-gun. Try him if you don't believe me."

"Okay," somebody said, so promptly it sounded like a joke.

A young cowpuncher wearing two low-slung six-shooters stepped away from the bar, the whiskey in him obviously talking loud. "That sounded like a dare. Us Texians don't take dares. Cut loose yore wolf, old Bat Dorn."

There was the usual exodus away from the probable line of fire, a few nimble ones making it out the front and back doors, or the windows.

"Thank a heap, Sarge," Dorn said as he stepped clear to face his challenger. As he expected, the young cowboy beat him to the draw by a mile. The kid was obviously so surprised by that himself that he didn't shoot.

"Take it easy, young feller," Dorn said smoothly. "You wouldn't want to kill an old guy like me." He took a step forward, hand held palm up. "Why not just hand over the six-shooter."

"Hell no!" the cowboy bawled. "I seen yore type down in Dodge. You ain't sweet-talkin' me outa my six-shooter. An' you ain't gittin' close enough to slug me like you did old Yahoo Dave. Fill yore hand."

Dorn didn't see much of an alternative. Sarge's advice was good as gold. Everyone, including the cowboy, expected him to fade for his quick-draw pistol tied down on his left leg. He had his regular job out before anyone knew it. The trouble was he didn't want to hurt the drunk kid. He'd been raised in a country that put no study into a quick draw but worshiped marksmanship because dueling—getting in one shot for sure—was a gentleman's sport. He recalled the duel, when he was only sixteen, that had got him expelled from VMU on the very day the Civil War started. He'd pinked old Calumet Yancey Drabo Tulliver right between the eyes. He could remember seeing the boy, no older than himself, fall backward. He'd gone to look at him and couldn't help but notice that most of the ball was still outside the skin. Either an underload or defective Yankee powder had saved Tulliver, except for a bad headache.

Now he covered the cowboy, very slowly. "Don't move, kid," he ordered.

But the kid did move. Dorn thought, I'll let him have one shot first. As it happened, he let him have six. The first shot almost went into the kid's own foot. The next was almost as bad. It hit the overhead lamp slightly ahead of where he stood. He was either blind drunk, scared out of his wits, or close to being the world's worst shot. Dorn started to laugh after the third shot. When the kid's gun was empty he was splitting.

"Damn you!" the cowboy yelled, tossing down that pistol and drawing his other.

Dorn thought, Enough is enough. He drew a steady bead on the kid's pistol and almost casually shot it from his hand. The effect was to sting hell out of the kid's hand, obviously. He was dancing around holding it with the other one, trying to get his breath.

The whole thing took maybe ten seconds. Dorn stepped up, retrieved the kid's still loaded pistol off the floor, and stuck it in his belt. Some of the other cowboys who had accompanied the "Texian" moved closer. Dorn quickly covered them.

"We ain't lookin' fer trouble, Marshal," one said. "The kid's my brother. I wanted to thank yuh fer not killin' the dang fool. I told him he was crazy to go up again' Bat Dorn, but he was crazy drunk."

"It's okay," Dorn said quietly. "Take him somewhere to sleep it off. And any of you that're stayin' here, check your guns with the bartender. That's my rule in town from now on. No guns except comin' and goin'. Pass the word."

He surveyed the crowd—what was still there. Others were returning cautiously, asking those who'd stayed what happened. He heard one being told, "Old Bat got a pistol out so fast nobody even saw him move." Dorn knew, of course, that they'd been looking the wrong direction, which had helped, as any magician would have attested. He casually returned to his place at the end of the bar. Sarge joined him, bringing a sergeant in uniform over.

"Bat," he said. "I'd like to introduce Sergeant O'Leary, sergeant major out at Fort Littleworth. Ben O'Leary."

Dorn shook hands with the sergeant, who said, "That was the finest piece of law work I ever saw. I'd like to buy you a drink."

"You wouldn't be offended if I had a cigar instead, would you?" Dorn said. "I try never to drink on duty." From the corner of his eye he saw Sarge roll his eyes up into his head. Dorn figured it wasn't exactly a lie, since this was the first time he'd been on duty as a marshal. But he knew what Sarge had been recalling—all the times he'd been pie-eyed when Sarge had covered for him with old Captain Thundifer, back in the Twenty-fifth.

Sergeant O'Leary was saying, "Tell me, Bat—I hope you don't mind my callin' you Bat—"

"Not at all."

"Anyhow. D'ya mind tellin' me why you used your right hand?"

Dorn laid on to just the right answer and thanked his guiding angel. He assumed a modest look. "I didn't want to take advantage of the kid," he said.

"Man, you really figured him close," O'Leary said admiringly.

"Yup!" was all Dorn said, lighting his cigar casually.

By the next day everyone at the fort would be aware of Sergeant O'Leary's opinion of Bat, from General George A. Dilly down to the newest recruit.

CHAPTER 4

IT was well after dark when Dorn returned to the tepee. He'd wondered if the two young squaws would still be there. They were, waiting faithfully with a good big fire going, roasting some of the remaining "slow elk." Waiting even more faithfully, if hope of gain is written off, was Old Paint, who wickered as he saw Dorn return. He walked over and stroked his muzzle and ears. Dorn wondered why the old horse had suddenly become so attached to him. He knew why the two squaws had. He'd treated them as a Southern-bred gentleman treated all women, and they reacted in kind.

He'd discovered that they both spoke more than enough English to get by on. They'd been sent East to the white man's Indian school and had later rebelled, for which he inwardly congratulated them. They'd gone back to the blanket and suffered the displeasure of the sanctimonious agent at the Fort Littleworth reservation. They'd been disowned by their families, who had no trouble making the choice between them with no rations and rations with no them. (That had been the agent's idea of suitable punishment for recusants.) The squaws thereupon had eloped with the two young bucks Dorn had sent packing. He'd half expected those two bucks to return to steal back their horses or to try to get their guns. He reminded himself to be on guard for that when he was in camp.

After filling his belly and enjoying a good cup of coffee made from the supply of Arbuckle's best he'd brought out from Hoak's Mercantile, he settled in for a good night's rest in the tepee. He reflected on all the things that had befallen him in just a couple of days. "What the hell," he told himself philosophically. "I'll probably get used to being in the middle most of the time."

Sarge was due out to his camp for breakfast. They planned to talk over the matter of establishing another saloon. Naturally it would have a gambling layout and probably dance-hall girls. Sarge had an eye for the ladies; he'd undoubtedly like having a bevy of his own. Since he'd told Sarge his two squaws were lookers, Dorn suspected that wasn't the least of the reasons he had insisted on having their confab in his camp.

Sarge showed up at dawn, wearing a blanket and feather. Dorn's first notice of his arrival was being awakened by some sort of scuffle. At first he thought it might be the two braves making a raid. Then he heard Sarge yelling, "Stop it, you pesky fleabag! Git! Git away!"

Dorn stuck his head out and caught the priceless spectacle of Sarge rounding the tepee at a high lope with Old Paint pacing behind, trying to nip him. Dorn headed off the horse on their next round. His two squaws came out to see what the fuss had been about, in their altogether, just as he himself was. They thought something was extremely funny. Dorn had a pretty good idea what it was. He hustled "it" into the tepee away from Old Paint's wrath.

"Are you tetched?" Dorn asked Sarge.

"Nope," Sarge said, puffing heavily. "Thought I'd don the appropriate attire. I read that 'don the appropriate attire' business in the New York papers. Classy, huh?"

"I can think of a place to stick that feather where it'd be classier. As for appropriate attire, you can see what us Injuns are wearin' this season."

"I couldn't help but notice that," Sarge admitted. "It looks a lot better on them than on you."

"Thanks. Now get that damn blanket and feather off so my hoss doesn't eat you. Obviously he's taken a dislike to Injun bucks since that one shot him the other day. Good thing for me. He'll be better'n a watch dog."

He went back outside where he heard the girls splashing in the river and plunged in to join them. "C'mon in," he yelled at Sarge. "The water's great."

"Took a bath last Saturday," Sarge said. "I'll get the fire started. I'm hungrier'n I'm dirty." It was a proposition that admitted of argument downwind from him. He'd brought a substantial pack of rations that had got distributed around the tepee in his mad career. He gathered them up, except the bag of flour, which Old Paint had got open and was delicately ingesting. The horse aimed a roundhouse kick at Sarge, perhaps just in case he really was a brave now masquerading as a white, then resumed eating the five-pound bag of flour.

"Pesky varmint," Sarge cussed him, but grudgingly recognized there was something about Old Paint's style that he admired.

By the time Dorn and his two "wives" were dressed, Sarge had the bacon on and coffee boiling. "Tell them two she-male Ay-rabs to take over," he growled. "Don't want to spoil 'em."

Dorn had already named the two "Ay-rabs" Mattie and Hattie. Mattie looked Sarge over carefully and concluded, "You're funny."

He looked surprised. Finally he recovered enough to grin. "So're you," he said, "and kinda cute, too, when you run around in your pelt."

She giggled.

"Hey, Dorn—I mean, Bat, your grace—did you know this one speaks English?"

"They both do. Had more schooling than you, I'd bet."

Sarge looked them both over with a little more respect. "How many pony's'll you take for this one?" he asked, indicating Mattie.

"Can't sell either one, old pal. Like I said, we're married. It's a sacred thing you likely wouldn't understand."

"Bull!" Sarge snorted. "I'll get 'em both in a poker game one of these days an' you know it."

Dorn grinned. "Maybe. Also perhaps. I never had two before. Everybody oughta. I'll have to take back what I used to believe about the Mormons."

After breakfast, sprawled in the shade on a buffalo robe apiece, with their stogies fired up, and sipping a second cup of coffee, Dorn and Hoak decided that things seemed just about right for a conference.

"I want the biggest, gaudiest place in town," Sarge said. "Money ain't no problem. I've screwed the damned army and Injun Bureau outa plenty by now. We want to do it up right. Always wanted my own whorehouse."

Both squaws giggled. Sarge looked around at them. "Git," he said. "Pesky red varmints. Your ears 're too sharp." To Dorn he said, "Send 'em out to exercise a couple o' horses or something."

"Good idea," Dorn agreed. He turned to them. "You two run the horses up into the mesa to graze. I'll come up and get you when I want you." When they were on their way Dorn said, "You sure we want gals in our place? They usually mean trouble."

"Kinda trouble I like," Sarge said. "Never had it regular in the army. I got an idea how to keep the best in the West. You run the likker and gamblin'. I'm gonna be in charge of the girls. We'll have a two-story place with the gals upstairs. Already ordered the boilerplate for the floors."

"Boilerplate? What the hell for?" Dorn asked.

"I don't want to get shot in bed by some galoot down in the saloon who gets likkered up and decides to pepper the ceiling."

After thinking it over briefly, Dorn could see that was a good idea. "Could give the place a bad name if someone got castrated by a forty-five slug," he allowed. "Boy, I'll bet that'd smart."

Sarge nodded. "About all you'd be good for after that is to sing soprano in the choir. Anyhow that won't be no problem. I can hardly wait to take away old Fancy Venere's business."

"Who the hell's Fancy Venere?"

"The Frog that runs the Bridgewater, first place when you come into town. I call it the Bilgewater. Got half the boys in the country callin' it that. But Venere's got the best business in town on accounta havin' a half-dozen whores—especially the Phoebe. She's some looker. We'll take a stroll down there and look the place over after a while." He suddenly guffawed. "Hey, why don't I order you as marshal to shut it down for bein' immoral? Then I could hire his gals. Save us bringin' in a bunch from St. Louis."

"Outside of him shootin' you, for which I wouldn't blame him under the circumstances, it sounds like a real great idea."

"He wouldn't dare shoot me with Bat Dorn around," Sarge said. "Why even Wild Bill hisself walked soft around—"

Dorn cut him off. "Save it for *Frank Leslie's* and the *Police Gazette*."

Sarge got a faraway look for a moment. "Yeah," he said. "That's it. You got it. I'll get yore phiz on the front of both of them papers as the pizenest varmint in the West. I was wonderin' what my next move should be to make you famous."

"If it works like yesterday I'm apt to get dead before I get famous."

"Pshaw. You handled it just right."

"The biggest darn piece of luck that ever happened. I almost shit my pants when the kid started shootin'."

"So? How do you know Wild Bill wasn't lucky, too? Only his Chinese laundryman could tell about the rest of it."

"Look," Dorn said seriously, "I'm figurin' on you hiring a real marshal as soon as you can swing it. I came here to run a saloon and gamblin' joint with maybe some boxing on the side. Got it? This Bat nonsense is all right for a little while, but I want to take my two wives buffalo hunting pretty soon. Nobody can beat a squaw at skinning."

"Okay, okay. Keep your shirt on for a while." Sarge sat up

straight, as if he'd just remembered something. "By the way, I sent a letter to Wyatt Earp down at Dodge. Maybe he'll come up and help you out with the marshaling if you throw them two squaws in with the bargain."

Dorn gave him a withering look.

"I know," Sarge grumbled. "It's sacred. Sacred my ass. Say, how'd you like to start our whorehouse with them two? I could give you half."

"You said we were gonna split fifty-fifty anyhow."

"Yeah, but I keep the books. We could really do it fair and square in this case."

They were interrupted by the growing noise of many horses approaching. Soon a company of cavalry came into view, heading in their direction. With the officer leading them were the two bucks whose outfit Dorn had appropriated.

"Oh-oh," he said to Sarge. "Big trouble. Those're the two bucks I kicked out of their camp. It looks like they maybe sweet-talked the army into rakin' their chestnuts."

Sarge eyed the cavalcade approaching. "If they did, they musta done a fine job of it—that's General Dilly himself leadin' the outfit."

"Not the famed boy general of the late, great war?" Dorn asked.

"You got him. Let me do the talking," Sarge said. Then to General Dilly, "Howdy, General, what brings you boys down here?"

The general pulled up and posed a trifle, causing his horse to curvet nervously and show off his horsemanship.

"Hello, Sarge," he replied brusquely. "A little matter of horse stealing and kidnapping." He eyed Dorn severely, then pointed at him. "Sergeant, we want this man."

A detail consisting of the sergeant and six men dismounted and approached Dorn purposefully.

"Careful, men," General Dilly cautioned. "He's deadly as a rattler."

"Wait a minute," Sarge protested. "That's Bat Dorn, my city marshal. What the hell's goin' on here?"

"We're taking your marshal to the fort in irons."

"The hell you are!" Sarge snorted. "Since when has the army taken up for slow-elkin' Injuns? Bat here caught them two skinnin' a Flying W beef. They tried to kill him. He later captured them and confiscated their outfit. We're holding it for the next term of circuit court."

The general smiled. "Sarge, you're one of the biggest loads of hot air I ever had to listen to. Now, I've got my duty to perform. Put that man in irons, men."

Dorn made no resistance, recognizing that fifty-to-one odds were pretty steep, even for Bat Dorn. They slipped the cuffs on him and took his pistols.

Sarge, who had the typical enlisted man's antipathy for officers, in spades, crooked a finger at the general.

"How about a private word with you, General, before you run off with my marshal?"

The general rode over to one side, and the two were in earnest conversation for a moment. Then the general, now slightly red in the face, spun his horse and yelled to his sergeant, "Turn Bat loose and give him back his guns. There's been a big mistake made here. And put those two bucks in the guardhouse and throw away the key when you get back to Fort Littleworth."

Dorn was duly amazed. When the cavalry patrol was out of hearing he asked, "What the devil did you say to him?"

Sarge grinned slyly. "I asked him how he'd like his pretty little wife to see the IOU's I hold from him for bein' a poor judge of cards and horses. She also thinks he don't cuss or drink. But she doesn't know her boy general like I do. Wait'll we get that whorehouse! I'll bet we find out he's got another little vice."

"Who hasn't?"

CHAPTER 5

THE Bridgewater struck Dorn as quite a place as western dives went. It was big, almost cavernous, due to a ceiling that must have been sixteen feet high, made of the usual ornately stamped tin. It had only a moderate number of bullet holes in it. Five cut-glass chandeliers and two dozen bracketed wall lamps were the building's sources of illumination, day and night. The mahogany bar which ran down one side of the room was at least sixty feet long. Beyond it were the roulette wheels and faro layouts, also a stage for variety acts at the very back. The rear portion had a second story with rooms for privately auditioning talent, as Dorn well understood.

"A second-class dump," Sarge growled, displaying the ultimate in prejudiced contempt, since his own dive existed, to date, only in his dreams.

Dorn held his tongue. He'd just been thinking it was the classiest place he'd seen since coming West.

"What do you think?" Sarge prodded him.

"I think you oughta buy us a cold beer, since I'm busted flat."

"Oh, I meant to fix that for you. Here." He gave Bat four quarters, keeping a perfectly straight face.

"Thanks," Dorn said, with an equally straight face. "Did anyone ever tell you you're a cheap such-and-so?"

"Uh-huh." By now they were at the bar. "Here comes the Frog," Sarge cautioned in a low voice.

Fancy Venere had an egg-shaped head, a receding hairline, a dapper black mustache, well waxed and curled at the tips, fat lips, and liquid brown eyes. He was of medium height and slender build, except for a small potbelly. Even now at midday he wore striped pants, a gray vest, and dark blue cutaway coat with tails and brass buttons. His fingers were festooned with diamond and gold rings. Dorn noted with disgust that his fingernails were varnished—also clean, a feature that invited instant suspicion on the frontier. Fancy reminded him of a doughboy everyone had called Fat Ed, which had been strange, many thought, because he wasn't fat and his name wasn't Ed.

"Ah, hizzoner the mayor," Fancy purred a greeting. "And I guess this would be the new marshal." He eyed Dorn with artfully feigned respect, though Dorn caught a touch of well-concealed sarcasm in his voice. A stray thought tempted him to suddenly yell "boo" at Venere. It might have triggered an interesting conversation, he imagined. When Fancy recovered from his shock he might ask, "What did you do that for?" And Dorn could reply, "Because it seemed like the thing to do to an oily little pismire trying to ingratiate himself with the big gun and at the same time be snide." This would have left Venere room to say very little except "Oh." But the psychological moment passed. Fancy was saying, "What'll it be, gents? It's on the house."

Dorn and Sarge each had a beer.

"C'mon back tonight for sure, boys," Fancy invited. "The Phoebe's got a new repertoire." Then he left.

"What makes him think we're leaving?" Sarge asked no one in particular, then added another vagrant thought. "You been to that sojer-boy college back in Virginny. What the hell's a repertoire? Is that anything like a strangulated hernia?"

Dorn eyed him in surprise. "Where'd you hear of a strangulated hernia?"

"I got a doctor's book."

"I'll bet," Dorn said. "To look at the pictures, right? What were you doin' readin' it?"

"The hell with you. All I asked was what a repertoire was."

"In this case it's an act. A new act."

"I liked her old one. In fact she doesn't need an act. If somebody'd just hide her clothes at about seven every night and send her out here to look for 'em for a half hour or so, they'd clean up all the money in the territory."

"That good, huh?"

"That good," Sarge said. "We gotta figure out how to steal her for our place."

"When we get it," Dorn added. "You want those four quarters back for my part of the investment?"

Sarge eyed him reproachfully. "Hell no. There's more where that came from. You think I'm a tinhorn or something?"

"Perish the thought. By the way, is there a bank in town?"

"I'm the bank. It's the safe down at the store. Why? You thinkin' of startin' a savings account with those four quarters?"

"Not exactly. I was thinking of heisting the bank so I could eat till payday."

Sarge fished into his vest pocket. He laid out five double eagles on the bar. "Here," he said. "It's a loan, so don't think I'm goin' soft."

"You want me to sign a note?" Dorn asked.

"No. I want you to come back to a poker table and help me clean Fancy outa a few thousand bucks. You ain't lost the touch with pasteboards, I don't reckon, as long as you stay sober."

"I never drink on duty," Dorn said. "And poker's more my kind of duty than playing Bat Dorn."

They were into the house for a substantial part of that few thousand when Sarge leaned over to Dorn and said in a very low voice, "Here comes the big artillery. Look out. They send her out so damn fools'll spend more time watching her teats than their cards. It's the Phoebe."

Dorn didn't look up right away, instead seeming to study his hand. He was aware of a green dress arriving just behind the player across from him. She put her hand caressingly on the back of the player's head. The man turned around, perhaps expecting Jack McCall, saw who it was, and got an instant dying-calf look. Dorn still hadn't looked at her face. What he could see was enough to keep an ordinary man busy for a while. He thought, she won't be able to give me that hair-twining treatment anyhow. He was sitting back-to-the-wall like good gunfighters are supposed to do. When he finally looked at her he got a considerable shock but managed to keep his poker face. She eyed him slumberously from a pair of violet eyes with long blond lashes. Her shimmering corn-silk hair was coiled on top of her head with enough left over for a long tress to hang down her back as well. She now drew it over her shoulder and twined it, giving Dorn an electric piercing appraisal. Her cleavage didn't hurt her act either. The usual word for her variety was "magnificent."

"I'll call and raise a hundred," he said, forgetting that the draw was over and he had a busted flush. On that hand he took his whipping like a man—or at least like a dying calf.

He was thinking rapidly, She doesn't recognize me or it would have shown on her face. Back then, of course, I was only a kid in her eyes. She sure has stood up mighty fine over the years. Lucky I changed my name when I headed west or that might've jogged her memory. She's surely been told I'm the redoubtable Bat Dorn. Then he wondered if maybe he was mistaking her for the other one. He pushed his hat low over his eyes and studied her while the house dealer ran the cards. No. He was sure it was her, the fabled beauty of the magnolia-drippin' sea islands, Sally Breckenridge Lacey, wife of Colonel Clay Beauford Romanza, the dashing cavalier, Jeb Stuart's favorite. Sally Romanza. He hadn't seen her since 1863. The thought occurred to him that being a femme fatale, she'd die if she thought someone at the table knew she had to be thirty-eight if she was a day. But she looked easily ten years younger. Comes from never having washed a dish and having played a zither instead of a washboard, he reasoned. And here she is a fallen woman. He wondered what poor old Clay would think. He could remember twenty or so duels Clay had fought over her virtue or something. He oughta have my job; he's cut out for it, Dorn told himself. Maybe the poor bastard'll come to town huntin' her, and Sarge can hire him to replace me. That is, if he hasn't drank himself to death. He remembered Clay as a good two-bottle man.

Sally Breckenridge Lacey Romanza—the Phoebe—hung around, trying a lot of contour contact on both Dorn and Sarge, who were now winning steadily. When she discovered that her wiles didn't seem to get the job done, she poutingly eyed them and said, "If you two take all our money I'll be out of a job."

"No, you won't," Sarge put in. "I'm puttin' in a joint across the street that'll make this one look puny. I'll put you on my payroll tonight and keep you on till it's finished."

"Thanks, Sarge," she warbled. "I'll feel better knowing I won't be out on the street." She smiled brilliantly, then took the smile, the cleavage, and a pair of swaying hips toward the rear of the room. "Come back for my act tonight, boys," she called over her shoulder.

Sarge pushed back his chair. "Well," he said, to no one in particular, "much as me and the marshal hate to leave big winners, that's the second invitation from the management we've had to come back. Can't very well do that unless we leave, can we?" He grinned lewdly. Normally the Bridgewater's big winners ended up out in the alley with a new bump of knowledge, but Sarge knew that Bat Dorn's reputation was going to get them out the door, down the street, and to his big safe, all in one piece. He fully savored the dealer's scowl.

"How about that?" Sarge said once they were outside. "I'll take that hundred back now."

Dorn peeled off a hundred from a roll of shin plasters so fat he'd had to put it inside his shirt. "Don't mind if I do," he said. "I expect you'll want interest."

"Next time maybe."

They put their rolls in the safe. Dorn had hit town broke. Bat Dorn was now a cool thousandaire. He counted his roll. His winnings came to $1,572.25. "At this rate," he said, "me and the girls can move outa the tepee."

"Got housekeeping rooms upstairs in the back," Sarge said. "Give you a good rate on 'em."

Dorn raised his eyebrows. "Like what?"

"Free. I'd like it known you're on the premises. Discourage thieves."

"Do you allow beer drinking?"

"I insist on it, especially if I'm up there inspecting the premises."

"By the way," Dorn said, changing the subject. "Do you think it was wise telegraphing our punch by telling the Phoebe you're gonna start a joint in competition with the Bilgewater?"

"Why not? Old Fancy can't do a damn thing to stop us."

"He'll try. I know the type. Sneaky. Could even be dangerous. I don't think his kind would hesitate to have you put away if it came down to it."

Sarge then changed the subject. "What did you think of the fabulous Phoebe?"

"She's all you said she was, and more." He decided not to tell how much more just yet. He wasn't sure why.

"You want to go down and take in her act tonight?" Sarge asked.

"Nope. I've got to get my gals off the mesa. They'll follow orders and be there all night if I don't. And don't you go down there to the Bridgewater either. Just a hunch. Don't go anywhere without me or some other good dependable man along."

"You tryin' to baby the old Sarge?"

"Yeah, as a matter of fact," Dorn said, "I am. And do me a favor. Lock the doors and go to bed. Or, better yet, spend the night down at camp with us."

"Shall I bring a tub of beer on ice?"

"Definitely."

"You plannin' to hog both them gals?"

"Definitely."

At Dorn's camp they moved into the tepee out of the evening's chill and were still amiably arguing over sleeping arrangements at midnight when Sarge settled the matter by passing out. Mattie tenderly covered him with a buffalo robe. Then she finished off her beer, holding up the bottle to the firelight.

"Beer great stuff," she said and passed out herself. Dorn carried her over and placed her in her bed beside Hattie, who'd folded earlier, closed the tepee flap, and rolled in. He was asleep almost at once. His last brief thought was, Old Paint'll stand guard—I hope.

CHAPTER 6

SALLY Breckenridge Lacey Romanza, the Phoebe, had been known as simply Breck to a short-lived generation of mooning swains. A good many of them died with their boots on from Bull Run to Appomattox. Others had thought of blowing their cavalier brains out when Sally had married Clay Romanza in 1863. Dorn, not then called Dorn as yet, had been one of them. He'd been Colonel Clay Romanza's regimental orderly sergeant. As such, Breck must have seen him on dozens of occasions without ever really seeing him. At least that's what he reasoned must have been the case, since she didn't appear to recognize him now. Of course he'd changed a great deal more than she had. In those days he couldn't even raise a respectable mustache. Now he had the required handlebar of the day. He remembered how, shattered as only an eighteen-year-old who thinks he is deeply in love can be shattered, he'd deserted the regiment so he wouldn't have to be agonized by the sight of his lost one. He'd joined Mosby's Rangers, intending to make a glowing reputation. And he had. But not as Dorn.

The Phoebe had been closeted with Fancy Venere shortly after she left Dorn and Sarge at the poker table. But she didn't let him in on Sarge's plan to start a competing joint across the street. She was a lady who played her cards close to her lovely, ample chest. Nor did she intend to tell him, at least not yet, that she knew who the new gun-swift marshal really was. Her poker face had been every bit as well trained as Dorn's. She not only remembered Colonel Romanza's lovesick orderly. She remembered that she'd watched him

38

covertly many times in those days, thinking he was the handsomest young man she'd ever seen, and the best built— a horrifyingly shocking thought for a young lady back then. She also recalled thinking it was a pity he wasn't rich. Or an officer. Because he was neither, she knew he was not for her. Her wealthy planter father would have never tolerated a lowbred son-in-law inheriting his fortune after he died. He was firmly wedded to the gentlemanly tradition of his class whereby a highbred son-in-law conned him out of his fortune *before* he died. The Civil War had aborted the usual cycle. He got the highbred con man in Colonel Romanza all right. But the war had swallowed the fortune by then.

Worse yet, Clay Romanza had turned out to be a hopeless sot. As soon as his days of glory evaporated, he had turned to the grape. Sally had watched his dissipating and prayed for divine intervention. It had come in the form of a stroke. For ten years now, Colonel Clay Beauford Romanza had been in the Tupelo sanitarium, where he was fed mush and milk three times a day by an attendant, since he himself always pushed it in his ear instead of his mouth, and wore diapers.

Breck's father, General Lacey, had been no stronger-willed than her husband. Faced with ruin he had also turned to the bottle. He was still alive, spent most of his time in the Keeley Institute, drying out. The Phoebe supported both of them, since her mother had died a few years earlier. She and her mother, unlike their menfolk, had bravely faced up to their plight after ruin overtook them. They'd opened a specialty house in Charleston, catering to the only class that had money—the Union officers of the Reconstruction forces. There she'd met the boy general, George A. Dilly, and had become his favorite. Later, she'd followed him to his various assignments, till his wife's father found out about her and cut off the general's allowance, breaking up the liaison. While holding Dilly in her arms as he sobbed himself to sleep after learning about the loss of this money, she felt her interest in him ebb. She recognized he was more concerned over the loss of this allowance than being without her. So she hadn't really cared when Dilly had left her in St. Louis; it had been final as far as she was concerned. Her mother had sent her funds to open her own parlor house there.

She soon had her eyes opened to the existence of the boomtowns in the West from listening to the men who'd come in to St. Louis for a toot. In those towns big money was being made in cattle, mining, and railroads. She'd tried a dozen towns, each for a few months as they'd boomed and peaked. But Warbonnet looked like a place that would pay off over the long haul. It had everything: the railroad coming in, the fort, an Indian agency, freighting, the growing cattle industry, and the mines in the nearby mountains. In ten years she could be independently wealthy and retire to the Riviera, or perhaps to Paris. In the meantime there was Dorn, as he was now known. Nothing stood in her way now. Sarge was planning to steal her, as he thought, from Fancy Venere. Well, she was planning to steal Dorn from Sarge. As yet she was unaware of his sacred union to Mattie and Hattie. But if she'd known of it, that wouldn't have deterred her. Breck always had been a determined girl. The Phoebe was a determined woman.

Dorn was, as yet, blissfully unaware of her plans. If he had known about them, he'd have been blissfully aware of them. Some long-banked fire he'd thought had died years ago had been relit when her eyes had met his that day. The archer had shot him years ago, and the arrow was still deeply imbedded in his heart. This old flame was to have a fateful impact on the early history of Warbonnet and Fort Littleworth, and the Tupelo sanitarium and the Keeley Institute, too.

CHAPTER 7

DORN locked his remuda, including Old Paint—who gave him an aggrieved look over the indignity—into Sarge's palisaded corral.

He was wondering if he should lock his harem into their new apartment as well. He'd noticed their look of avid interest as they'd passed through the store, like collectors in an antique shop. He could envision wings on some of his $1,572.25 winnings from the Bilgewater. Then an alternative suggested itself. His feeling about his celestially conceived nuptials didn't appear nearly as sacred when balanced against hard cash. He thought he'd let nature take its course. No telling who might trade what to whom for what while Sarge was minding the store and he was patrolling Warbonnet. Mattie's and Hattie's externals underwent a remarkable change in just a few days, without denting his bankroll a cent. They shucked their buckskins and moccasins in favor of gingham, button shoes, ribbons, and even sunbonnets. He made no comment on this. Sarge soon began to whistle as he worked. He'd also acquired the habit of eating with Dorn and the girls, who were both turning into passable cooks of "civilized" chuck, given something to work with.

The materials for Bat's Place had started to arrive on Yahoo Dave's wagon trains. Sarge had contracted the work out to Fritz Brautigam, a master builder he'd imported from St. Louis. He invited Dorn to witness the ceremony of his turning the first spadeful of dirt for the basement.

Brautigam had the street full of workers, telling them off to various jobs. "Jeezuz," Sarge observed to Dorn as they

41

came down the street, "I told him I wanted the place done before winter, but I didn't expect him to hire an army."

"You mean you didn't swindle the army and Injun Bureau out of quite enough?" Dorn asked unhelpfully.

"Of course I did. But no damn Kraut's gonna get rich off me."

The street was full of teams with wagons, teams with slip scrapers, at least two dozen men with shovels, a couple of surveyors, and unspecified others, perhaps merely curious onlookers. Several newly arrived freight wagons were being unloaded on the empty lot across the street next to the Bridgewater. Fancy Venere was outside in his shirtsleeves, smoking a cigar and supervising the freighters. That touched off Sarge. He stormed over to Venere, ignoring Fritz Brautigam, who came forward to greet him.

Confronting Venere, Sarge bawled, "What the hell you think you're doin'?"

Venere asked suavely, "What do you mean what am I doing? Anyone can see what I'm doing. I'm telling these men where to stack these building materials."

Sarge got a trifle red. "What's it to you where they put my stuff?" he roared.

"Nothing," Venere said, postponing his moment of triumph. "*You* can have *your* material put anywhere you want it. This is *my* material and *my* lot."

Sarge looked as nonplussed as Venere had hoped he would. "What the hell're you gonna build?" he asked.

"Well," Venere said, dragging it out, "I figured the town could use a good honest general store. So I'm buildin' one."

Sarge was completely at a loss for words. Finally he said lamely, "What's the matter with the store we got?"

Venere said, "Nothing yet. It's the best in town. So far."

Sarge knew when he'd been euchred, though he didn't like to admit it. He turned on his heel and rejoined Dorn. The marshal had been watching a figure partially concealed by the lace curtains of a second-floor window of the Bridgewater. At first he'd thought whoever it was might represent a threat. Then he made out a woman. She was very scantily attired. He was sure his eyes were playing tricks on him when she leaned forward, showing an immense amount of cleavage, and smiled and blew him a kiss. He saw the long blond hair swirl as she saucily spun from view, waving a delicate hand as she did. Breck. It could have been no one else. He felt a trifle weak in the knees and was assailed by all sorts of sensations here and there where they didn't do him any harm. His pulse had quickened by about half again. He felt just like he had as a green youth when Breck's carriage used to deposit her at Col. Clay Romanza's headquarters.

He wondered what that scene in the window was all about. He sure planned to find out as soon as possible. The question was how to go about it. He was annoyed when Sarge interrupted this pleasant speculation.

"Did you hear what that little pismire said?" Sarge blurted as he rejoined Dorn.

"I'm afraid I did. What do you aim to do about it?"

"Not much I can do about it. I'll have to think it over."

"Obviously a tit-for-tat move," Dorn said. "If you're worried about it you might make a deal to call off our saloon."

Sarge gave him a pained look. "Not on your tintype. I got enough dough to cut prices and break him if I have to."

"Maybe there's enough business to go around," Dorn suggested.

"Of course there is. But I don't want *him* to get any of it. I'll think of something." Then he turned to Brautigam. "What's this army for? You got twice as many men as you need," Sarge grumbled.

"Half of them are to build Mr. Venere's store."

That was one too many for Sarge. "Are you building his store too?"

"Of course. Is something wrong?"

Sarge was silent for a moment. "Naw," he said. "At least it ain't your fault if there is." To Dorn he said, "C'mon. Let's get out of here."

"What about the ceremonial spadeful of earth?" Brauti-gam asked.

"Stick the ceremonial spadeful, and the ceremonial spade. I need a drink." He spun on his heel and stalked off. Dorn had a hard job to keep the grin off his face as he dutifully caught up to his friend.

"I'll burn down the son of a bitch's store as soon as it's up," Sarge said.

"I'll have to arrest you."

"I'll fire you."

"You'll be in jail."

"I'll fire you anyhow."

They proceeded back to the store in silence. Once inside Sarge headed for the stockroom, pulled a bottle of hundred-proof Kentucky bourbon out and slugged down that drink he needed. He passed the bottle to Dorn.

"How much would you take to shoot that bastard Venere?" he grumbled. Then, getting no answer, he nodded resign-edly. "Okay, I know you ain't built that way. What a shame Wild Bill's dead. Do you suppose I could get Wyatt Earp to do it?"

Dorn took a pull at the bottle. "If you ask me," he said, "you're gettin' all het up over nothing, if there's plenty of business to go around."

"Yeah, but I hate Venere's guts."

"Like him maybe playin' house with the Phoebe?" Dorn had almost said "Breck."

"That, too. Think of that little terrier being with that—"

Dorn thought that over. He began to wonder how much Sarge would have been willing to pay to have Venere shot. He'd learned long ago that there was nothing like the blessed spirit of thrift involved in arranging to get paid for some-thing you aimed to do anyhow. Actually, although he'd had to kill a lot of people, he knew he was dreaming. He couldn't shoot a man in cold blood. But the thought of watching Venere kick his last was a pleasant one nonetheless.

As Sarge tossed off another big snort, both men heard hoofbeats approaching the loading platform out back, then boot heels on the planks. Cantoon entered the room. He obviously had a lot on his mind and almost spilled it before he saw Dorn.

"Oh—hi, Bat," he said. Then, to Sarge, "Is it okay to talk? We got a problem."

"Sure," Sarge said. "Old Bat and me ain't got any secrets between us."

That's what you say, Dorn thought. He knew Sarge wasn't simple enough to really believe that.

"Tell me, Sarge, what do I do for a living?" Cantoon asked.

Sarge looked amazed. "Why, hell, you steal cattle," he finally said.

"Right," Cantoon agreed. "The best damn rustler between Canada and the Rio Grande."

"Right," Sarge agreed.

"And what are you expecting me to deliver this week?"

"Some swiped cows."

"Would you be put out a lot if I didn't?"

"Hell yes. Unless you have a powerful good reason."

"Well, I got a good excuse—kinda."

"What happened?"

"You ain't gonna believe this."

"Try me."

"Some son of a bitch rustled my herd."

"When?" Sarge asked.

"Last night. We had 'em penned up good in a box canyon, so me 'n' the boys come uptown to the Bilgewater. When we got back they was gone."

Sarge looked at him for a while nonplussed. Then he started laughing. Dorn couldn't help but grin himself. "That's rich," Sarge was finally able to get out.

"It ain't funny," Cantoon grumbled. "I gotta think about my reputation."

"Well, I'm sure not gonna tell anybody," Sarge said. "I'm sure Bat won't. You were really pretty lucky."

"How in blazes do you figure that?"

"Suppose they'd been swiped after you sold 'em to me? I'd have been out some money. In this case you ain't out a cent. It's better 'n insurance. You got the easy end of this business."

Cantoon gave Sarge a leery look. "You didn't swipe them cows, did you?"

Sarge looked pained. "Of course not. What do you think I am, a crook? Don't I always pay you at least half what cows are worth?"

Cantoon looked apologetic. "Yeah. You always do. It's just that gettin' rimmed at my own game bends me outta shape."

"Here," Sarge said, offering him the bottle. "This'll make you feel better."

After Cantoon left, Sarge said, "Somebody's been watchin' my affairs a little too close, I think. Probably that bastard Venere. What'd be easier than for him to have his own crowd boost that herd, knowin' Cantoon and his boys were down at the Bilgewater instead of out keepin' an eye on it?"

"How would he know Cantoon had a herd in the first place?" Dorn asked.

"I don't know. Probably followed him. Maybe one of Cantoon's crowd is sellin' us out to Venere. I wouldn't put it past any of them. At least I'm not out anything but time. Cantoon'll have some more cows in a week or two."

"How come Cantoon doesn't sell directly to the Injun Agency instead of to you?" Dorn asked.

"Everyone knows he's a rustler. I buy my stock. There's a big difference," Sarge observed piously.

"Don't any of the cattlemen follow him when he runs off their stuff?"

"It's a big country," Sarge said. "It'll come to that, though. More herds comin' up from Texas every year. It'll get so an honest man can't make a living anymore. That's another reason I want to open our joint. It'll offset having to go out of the beef-supplying business. I figure we got one more good year rustlin' and that's all."

Dorn had trouble keeping a straight face over that "honest man" not being able to "make a living anymore." He watched for any sign that Sarge was being slyly funny, but he appeared perfectly serious about it. That's what Dorn liked about the old boy. He was guileless, almost.

CHAPTER 8

DORN hadn't forgotten Breck. In fact she'd been on his mind almost continually since he'd seen her at the window down at the Bridgewater. He had a great deal of company in this respect around Warbonnet. If the local mental telepathy had been like a telephone system, most of the male numbers would have been busy all the time on account of Breck. Dorn was planning to "casually" drop into the Bilgewater on his appointed rounds as soon as possible.

His boots were purposefully churning up small dust clouds, making tracks down the alley in that direction, when he ran into a little girl with a smudge on her nose. She was a remarkably pretty girl—he'd guess about five or so—with long chestnut pigtails. She carried a small pail in one hand and held the hand of a skinny boy, obviously younger, in the other. He also carried a small pail.

"Hi," Dorn greeted the pair. He stopped and they stopped. "Been berry pickin', I guess," he added. "Yer maw gonna make a pie?"

The girl eyed him uncertainly with huge dark eyes in a pale face. She was obviously debating whether to trust this smiling stranger. Dorn's honest face won out. Besides, young as she was, the girl knew her family was in deep trouble and needed help. She said, "Ma can't make a pie—she's too sick."

"Aw," he said. "That's too bad. Did your paw get a doctor for her?"

"He don't live with us anymore," the little boy said.

"He's dead," the girl said softly.

"Gone to heaven, Ma said," the boy chimed in. "We all miss him."

48

"Look," Dorn said. "I'm the marshal." He pointed to his badge. "I'm around to help out people in trouble." He'd forgotten all about where he'd been headed.

The little girl nodded. "You're like a policeman," she said.

"Right. So why don't you take me down to your maw and I'll try to help out. My name's Dorn, by the way."

"Mine's Annie and this is my brother, Abe," she said. "C'mon, I'll show you where we live."

He followed her to the edge of town to a squalid little shack in a weedy yard. It was so small that a door and one window almost covered its whole weathered board front. Two windowpanes were broken, stuffed with burlap sacks to keep out the weather. The girl led the way inside. No one was in the front part. A coarse piece of muslin screened off the rear. Dorn could see the iron legs of a bed beneath it.

"Annie, is that you?" a low female voice asked from behind the partition. "I was worried, you were gone so long."

"We got lots of berries," Annie said. "And someone's here."

The voice changed. "Who?" There was apprehension in its tone.

"Mr. Dorn. He's come to help."

"Tell him to go away. We don't need any help." There was an uncertain note in the voice. Dorn could imagine a proud woman might be ashamed of her appearance and of their obvious poverty and squalor.

"I'm the marshal, ma'am," he said. "Annie told me you were sick. I'm here to help. I'm gonna get you a doctor." He paused.

"We don't have any money to pay a doctor," the woman said. "We don't have any money at all."

"That don't matter," Dorn assured her. "No Christian community leaves people in your shape. You shoulda told someone. Somebody shoulda noticed before now. I'll be right back."

He hotfooted back down to Sarge's and told him about the needy family. "You know anything about 'em?" he asked.

Sarge appeared a trifle put out. "You oughta know if I did I'd of helped out before now. Let's get some grub together for 'em. I'll get Doc Carruthers and meet you down there. Take one of our squaws along. Injun gals're good at nursin'."

Dorn let that "our" squaws slide by under the circumstances. He rounded up Mattie and a big sack of groceries and headed back down to the shack where Annie lived. The little girl met him at the door.

"I was comin' to get you," she said in panic. "I think Maw died. She was tryin' to be up when you came with the doctor." The girl was losing a brave struggle to hold back her tears.

He hastily went inside. The woman was prostrate on the floor. Little Abe was hugging her, crying. "Please don't die, Ma," he gulped out between sobs.

Dorn felt for the woman's pulse. It was still beating. "She's not dead," he reassured the kids. "C'm'ere, Mattie, and help me get her back on the bed."

They tenderly deposited her in bed. Mattie placed the woman's head gently on the pillow and smoothed her hair. Her face was an older version of Annie's, pale and fine-boned, and her hair was the same rich chestnut color with a few faint streaks of gray. She reminded Dorn of the idealized pictures he'd seen of angels on calendars.

Mattie studied her intently, then turned to Dorn with a concerned look. "She's just hungry, Dorn. I know the look. I ought to. I'll fix some grub." She looked around for utensils or a stove. None were in sight.

"Where do you cook?" she asked Annie.

"Outside," Annie told her. She led the way out the back door. There was a rude stone campfire setup with a grill on top. A pile of twigs and some buffalo chips stood beside it. A pot and frying pan hung on the outside wall. Tin plates and cups were stacked on a small shelf. Mattie thought, Huh, the whites treat some of their own people as bad as they do us.

"Where do you cook when it rains?" Mattie asked Annie.

"It ain't rained since we had to sell the stove," Annie said. "Besides we haven't had anything to cook for a long while."

Inside Sarge had arrived with Doc Carruthers. The doctor had heard enough from Sarge that one look confirmed his suspicions. "Malnutrition," he snapped. "Helluva thing to happen in a civilized community. Hasn't the woman any friends?"

"She has now," Sarge affirmed. "Woulda had long before now if I'd have heard about her."

The doctor put some smelling salts under the woman's nose. She winced, then opened her eyes.

As Dorn had thought they would be, her eyes were big and dark, like her daughter's.

"Who're you?" she asked.

"The doctor," Carruthers said. "You're gonna be all right. Don't worry about a thing. We'll see that the kids are okay, too."

She closed her eyes, a small smile on her face. "Thank God," she whispered.

Outside, Mattie was already seeing to Annie's malnutrition. They were both working on the peppermint candy Dorn had tossed into the bag of provisions as Mattie got a fire going. Abe had just gone out and was helping them, especially with the candy. Doc Carruthers would have had a conniption fit. His prescription would have run more to hot broth for starters.

Sarge and Dorn arranged to move Annie's family to a more comfortable cottage owned by Sarge. The family's name was O'Neal. They left Mattie there as nurse. "She can spell off with Hattie, I reckon," Dorn said. "Is that okay with you?" he asked Mattie.

"Sure. They need help."

Dorn had never known how good-hearted Indians were till he'd inherited his two wives. He'd seen how close Mattie was to tears when she'd first seen Mrs. O'Neal and helped him get her back in bed. He wished more whites would react the same to the plight of Mattie's people, most of whom were often in the same condition, or worse. The trouble is, he thought, so few know about it. The army had always fed and doctored its Indian prisoners, especially the women and children. Soldiers were always quick to forgive and show mercy as soon as the fighting was over. He and many of his comrades had at times willingly gone on short rations, or none, to feed starving Indian prisoners even though they knew the Indians, in their shoes, would have tortured them to death.

As they walked back to his store Sarge said, "She's Square Deal O'Neal's widow. Everybody figured she'd go home to her folks back in Illinois. Musta took sick and run outa money."

"Did she have any money in the first place?" Dorn asked.

"I dunno," Sarge admitted glumly. "O'Neal worked for Fancy Venere, so I didn't want anything to do with him."

"What did he die of?"

"What do you think? He was a gambler. Hit a hot streak and somebody killed him one night on his way home. When we found him his pockets were empty."

"Any suspects?"

"About a hundred, I'd guess. Anybody he took money off of."

Dorn couldn't forget the grateful look O'Neal's widow—her name was Marie—had given them after Doc managed to get some nourishment into her. Dorn somehow felt she'd meant the message especially for him, although she'd felt obliged to thank them all.

Within an hour, Dorn and Sarge had moved the family into the small, clean cottage at the edge of town and had seen to it that they got settled in.

Annie had followed Dorn out in the yard and taken his big hand in her own warm, soft little one. She'd looked up at him with her big, dark eyes and said, "Ma says she prayed, and God sent you. Are you ever comin' back?"

He'd smiled and squeezed her hand. "I'll be back, honey," he said. "Soon."

Somehow the matter of Breck had faded from his mind.

When he thought of her again it didn't seem so important to go right down to the Bilgewater.

I'll think about it first, he told himself. Bein' God's ministering angel gives a feller a new outlook on things.

When Annie had told him he was the answer to a prayer, something about her believing, childish look had caused a strange, creepy feeling to run up and down his spine. No one had ever told him that, at least not anyone who believed it entirely. Besides he'd always been a softie for kids, especially little girls with huge, dark, trusting eyes.

"If I'd had a sister," he told Sarge, "I'd have liked one just like that little Annie."

"How about a daughter?" Sarge asked.

"That, too. But I ain't the marryin' type."

"That's what we all said," Sarge sighed.

Dorn looked him over carefully for signs of leg-pulling. "You been married and held out on me all these years?"

"Hell no," Sarge said. "But I'm thinkin' about it."

"Who's the likely victim?" Dorn asked.

"I ain't sure."

"What do you mean you're not sure?" Dorn asked.

"Well, I'm waitin' to see which one of them Injun wives you get rid of first. Then I'll marry that one."

Dorn guffawed. "Suppose I get rid of 'em both?"

Sarge eyed him slyly. "Then I'll marry 'em both. Legal, too—none of that sacred conceived-on-high bull shit like you been givin' me."

Dorn laughed at Sarge's seriousness, especially since bigamy was scarcely legal.

"Well," he said, "if you feel that way, Sarge, you can have either one that'll have you."

"Thanks—I think. Waddaya mean 'that'll have me'? I'm the richest son of a bitch in camp. That cuts ice with squaws."

"So hop to it," Dorn said. "I'll be best man."

"If yer asked," Sarge said. "If yer asked. Now, how about gettin' out and patrollin' town like I'm payin' you to do?"

So, three hours after he'd set out the first time for the Bilgewater, Dorn found himself slowly retracing his steps, deep in thought. What do I have to lose? he argued with himself. I've been in love with Breck most of my life. I wonder if she'd marry me. He almost laughed at himself.

Marriage hadn't been exactly what he'd had in mind earlier. But somehow that look in little Annie's eyes had made him question all of his former ways.

Do you suppose I'm gettin' religion at my age? Dorn asked himself. Or worse yet, morals?

Those were solemn thoughts.

CHAPTER 9

BRECK had just happened to be at her window to observe Dorn's approach. She quickly checked her appearance at her vanity and just happened to make one of her famous entrances down the stairs after she peeked to see if he was inside. She gave him enough time for his eyes to adjust from the bright sunlight outside. Halfway down the stairs she stopped and surveyed the room regally with her violet eyes, then smiled as she pretended to discover his presence. She gracefully crossed the room to where he stood.

All of his old feeling for her swarmed through him. Almost. Perversely, a picture of little Annie's trusting eyes swam between them. He suddenly felt ashamed of what he'd been thinking. Instead, he switched to wondering what their kids would look like if he married Breck.

Breck had devoted considerable thought to this meeting. For example she would have liked to toss Dorn over her shoulder and carry him up to her boudoir, but doubted she was strong enough. He stood six feet two and probably weighed one hundred and ninety-five pounds, she guessed. Obviously strategy would be necessary.

"Good morning, Marshal," seemed like a good opener, especially purred out in a husky half-whisper. At least Dorn thought so.

"Mornin', ma'am," he said. He'd decided to delay letting on that he knew who she was and let her tip her hand first if she wanted to.

She eyed him speculatively, then said, "Something your big sidekick, Sarge, said the other day interested me. Won't you come up and join me for breakfast so we can talk privately?"

Dorn had had breakfast about five o'clock, but thought he'd neglect mentioning it, since he'd devoted considerable thought to maneuvering her upstairs alone. "Why not?" he agreed.

She gloated to herself. He was going to be as easy as the rest of the simpletons. Somehow, though, she felt a little disappointed, a condition doomed not to last long on that specific count.

Upstairs he discovered that she had an extensive layout of her own, which surprised him a little. He'd expected a simple bedroom. She escorted him into a wide parlor with a marble fireplace, its hearth now shuttered behind ornate hinged brass doors; divans and chairs were liberally distributed around, sided by marble-topped tables with lace doilies, some covered with books and magazines such as *Godey's Lady's Book*. Bric-a-brac stood on shelves and in display cases all over the room. The floor was carpeted heavily in an expensive Brussels of subdued floral design. Drapes and hinged shutters of expensive dark walnut enclosed the windows. Original oils graced the walls, exquisitely matching the embossed baby-blue flowered wallpaper. The whole was set off by two cut-glass chandeliers pendent from a high ceiling.

A big orange-and-white tomcat occupied the windowsill. The cat glanced around once to see who his mistress was chatting with, blinked once at Dorn, and returned his attention to the street below. Dorn liked cats and knew enough about them to ignore this one. He bet himself it wouldn't be five minutes before the cat couldn't stand being ignored any longer and came over to investigate him.

Breck offered Dorn half of the love seat and occupied the other side herself.

"It's been a long time, hasn't it?" she opened.

He knew what she meant. In fact, he expected she wouldn't try to conceal her identity, since a large framed photo of husband, Clay Romanza, was plainly displayed on the mantel. He nodded. "A real long time," he agreed.

"Were you shocked to find me in a place like this?" she asked, watching him closely.

"I was shocked at finding you in the West," he admitted. "Much less here."

"A woman has to survive," she said.

"Where's Clay?" he asked.

She told him her husband was in a sanitarium, without concealing any of the sordid aspects of the affair.

"And your folks?"

She was equally frank in telling him about them. Then she said, "I don't know why I should burden you with all that. I guess because you stepped in from that lovely old world. God, how young and carefree we all were before the war." She paused, then added ruefully, "And dumb."

He shrugged. "We are what we have to be. Eventually we all outgrow our past."

She eyed him speculatively, some secret thought causing her violet eyes to grow suddenly dark. "Did you outgrow yours?" she asked. "I always knew you were in love with me. Did you outgrow that?"

He laughed over her frankness. "Was it so obvious?"

"A woman knows—even as young as I was," she said.

"Breck," he said, "everyone was in love with you. Even Bobbie Lee."

To his surprise she blushed. His remark had recalled to her a stroll in the moonlight with Lee, the Confederacy's Marble Image—out behind Mrs. Chesnut's house in Richmond. The great man had impulsively kissed her several times, and she recalled her shock at feeling him pressed against her and discovering that he was just like ordinary mortals. She was thinking that she probably could have got those dignified gray trousers of his off out there in the bushes, since Lee must have needed a woman badly. That thought caused the blush. Her afterthought was that she should have. The Phoebe, like others of her trade, was of a generous nature. Unfortunately, the Old South's strict upbringing had blighted the development of many potentially generous young ladies. Breck had been lucky in a way. Necessity had made of her a whole woman. She had learned to be perfectly natural around the men she liked.

A magic aura of the past surrounded them for a golden moment. Before Dorn realized what was happening, they were somehow naturally and innocently embracing and kissing. She was all he had expected, warm and responsive, breathing heavily in a very short while. Then the waiter bringing up breakfast pounded loudly on the door. Dorn and Breck drew apart, eyeing each other in a sort of dazed surprise. The knock came again and shattered the precious spell.

"Damn breakfast," she said.

He couldn't have agreed more. Reluctantly she rose and let the waiter in with a cart covered by a white tablecloth.

"I'll take it," Breck told him and rolled the cart toward the adjoining room. Dorn followed. By then he was not at all surprised to find a dining room as well-appointed as the room they'd just left.

Dorn thought, Fancy Venere takes good care of his private stock. He wondered where the oily little Frenchman was that she felt free to entertain another man like this. He didn't really care, however. If he ended up having to shoot Venere, he had the consolation of knowing Sarge would undoubtedly pay him a bonus. He might even defray the funeral expenses that the code required of noted gunfighters such as Bat Dorn. Wild Bill always gave his victims a decent burial, he recalled. It lent a certain classy touch of noblesse oblige to such affairs, the mark of the professional.

Breck left breakfast cooling on the tray. She was perfectly direct about it. "Between the three of us," she observed with a deft smile, "I'd rather let breakfast cool off."

He considered that an eminently practical observation. She stood in front of him waiting, and he did not disappoint her, enfolding her in a long kiss, then another. "You haven't seen the rest of my apartment," she told him. "C'mon." She led him by the hand into the bedroom. It was dominated by a huge canopied bed.

She turned and met him inside the door, placing her hands on his shoulders, gently restraining him for a moment. She looked down pensively for a few seconds, then up into his eyes, giving him the full treat of those tender violet orbs, now almost black with passion. He was by then suitably conditioned for the woodpeckers to go to work on his head, which was just what she'd had in mind.

"I used to think you were the handsomest man in Virginia," she confessed in a soft whisper. It made sense to him. So had he—possibly even in the Confederacy.

She led him to the bed and seated herself on the edge, patting a spot beside her invitingly. He sat down. This was all going the way he'd hoped and planned. He ought to be blessing his lucky stars, but somehow something was out of place. He looked at her, carefully masking his doubts. She was more than he'd hoped for, lovelier than ever with the poised beauty of a mature woman. He asked himself, What's missing? What more could I ask? The answer came to him as a revelation. He'd never voiced such a thought to himself before that day: This whole thing is immoral! But he was trapped. He liked Breck. Perhaps still loved her. He couldn't disappoint her now. Besides he'd look like a fool in the bargain. It was too new to him. He hadn't yet achieved that pinnacle of nobility that truly good men were capable of mounting—a willingness to look like a dunce in the cause of morality. The Christian world encompasses no greater height of dedication. (And, of course, heights of dedication are all such men usually mount.)

He recalled the old Roman saying: The gods frown on him who is summoned to a woman's couch and does not obey. He told himself that he would obey and pray for forgiveness later.

"The bootjack is under the bed," she said. He readily

found it next to the pink-flowered chamberpot and the cat, which had followed them.

Breck watched him undress, a look of passion capturing her face. "Hurry," she urged. "I want you to undress me too. I can hardly wait for you to hold me in your arms."

In the middle of the huge bed they kissed without restraint, wildly devouring each other's lips. As he began to savor Breck, nearly losing himself in this abandoned moment, a picture of little Annie's big, innocent, trusting eyes again pervaded his mind. The effect on him, devastating, almost changed his mood. He hoped Breck hadn't noticed it, but he knew elephants didn't fly.

She had known a lot of men, though, even some sensitive ones and she giggled. "Silly, you got too anxious. Relax awhile." She rolled over and smiled up at him. "Didn't that ever happen to you before?" she asked.

"Only once," he admitted. "The first time. I was a kid and scared to death."

She grasped the problem and ministered to it with an understanding touch. "Fine wine," she said, "is made slowly. And savored the same way. Besides," she added, "I found out long ago you can't push spaghetti uphill. And lecturing it sure doesn't help either."

He guffawed. "Breck," he said, "you've sure turned out to be a peach. How would you like to get married?"

She looked startled. "I am married, remember?" Then she pulled him toward her.

Much later as he was buttoning his trousers, he asked Breck, "Suppose old Fancy had walked in on us?"

"He's in St. Louis," she said. "Buying groceries and hardware for the new store."

For his part, Dorn fervently prayed he'd stay there—and, of course, he also prayed for forgiveness. He thought, I'll get the hang of this morality business yet, and if I can't manage that, I'll settle for faith.

He never did discover what business she'd wanted to discuss with him when she'd first invited him upstairs.

It'll keep, whatever it was, he told himself.

The cat reached out and playfully batted his foot as he was putting on his boots. Dorn reached down and batted back at him. Noticing this, Breck said, "He loves to play."

"What's his name?"

"Cupid."

CHAPTER 10

SARGE Hoak was not the sort of fellow to passively allow someone to rustle cattle from his rustler. His fertile mind had been at work on how to catch the big crook, whoever he was. He was particularly irked to hear that the Fort Littleworth Indian agent, Jack Crumm, had undoubtedly bought that particular twice-purloined herd. Part of his scheme to get information consisted of playing Jack Crumm and General Dilly off against each other. The only time the two communicated personally was at Sarge's celebrated poker sessions. The rest of the time they only addressed each other by official letter. Accordingly, Sarge scheduled a Saturday night poker and booze session. In addition to Crumm and Dilly he invited Major Bulstrode, a retired English officer who was post sutler, and Major Pizza of General Dilly's command, a monumental toper and poker addict. Pizza had fought with Garibaldi in Italy—usually over women.

Naturally Sarge planned to include Dorn in the game as his card mechanic. He knew that Dorn could make cards come out of a deck—or anywhere—in any order he needed them, at least when he was sober. They were seated together now, casually smoking cigars while waiting for the others. The card room was on the second floor of the store, as were their living quarters. It wasn't as ornate as the second floor of the Bridgewater, but not too bad for a frontier town. The room was tastefully decorated, although it had a linoleum floor rather than Brussels carpets. Obviously Sarge had had some good advice from someone about fixing it up. The main piece of furniture was a large round poker table covered with green felt, with trays on the edges for chips and glasses. Captain's chairs with comfortable arms and high backs were set around the table. There was an overhead chandelier with a half-dozen kerosene lamps in it.

Sarge handed Dorn a small package. "Three guesses what's in this," he said.

Dorn turned it over in his hand, hefting it for weight. "Another four quarters?" he guessed.

"Oh, crap," Sarge said. "Open it."

Inside was a shiny new star. Dorn eyed it critically. "Where'd you get this, some hock shop? I'm marshal, not deputy sheriff."

"You're both now," Sarge told him. "And as soon as I can manage it you'll be a U.S. deputy marshal."

"Thanks a heap, old buddy," Dorn said. "That's like having three targets where my suspenders cross instead of only one. What the hell's the big idea?"

"For one thing I need you to catch some cattle thieves."

"How about starting with Cantoon?" Dorn suggested.

Sarge didn't bother to answer, or even grimace. "You need jurisdiction out in the country," he said.

Dorn snorted. "I need three replacements is what I need."

"You're too modest. Don't forget you're famous down South."

"Yeah, and if you keep at it I'll be dead up North. Brother, the sacrifices I make for my friends."

Sarge remembered something. "By the way," he said, "a little bird told me you spent a lot of time upstairs at the Bilgewater. You got a friend up there you're makin' sacrifices for?"

"You told me to patrol the town," Dorn said. "I figured it wouldn't hurt to get acquainted in one of the big trouble spots."

"Sure," Sarge snorted. "Just bein' a smart marshal, right? If them Injun gals catch on that you spent a couple hours with the Phoebe, the sacrifice you'll make is your hide. You'll end up singing soprano. By the way, how was that stuff?"

Dorn smiled blandly. "I wouldn't know. We had breakfast and talked business. My guess would be she wants to make sure she has a job if you actually do break Fancy Venere, so she decided to butter up your old sidekick."

"Hell, if that's her game, she'd best invite me up to breakfast."

"I'll tell her when I see her again, if I do."

Sarge laughed. "Haw! That's rich! *If* you see her. You'll probably be down there patrollin' first thing in the morning."

Further conversation was forestalled by the arrival of the poker contingent from the fort. Jack Crumm was with them. Sarge introduced Dorn all around, even to General Dilly again, this time formally.

"I've heard a lot about you," Major Pizza said. "You're famous down South." He eyed Dorn amiably. "I'm famous in Italy. That's why I'm here." He didn't exactly suggest there could be a parallel between his fame and Dorn's, but the implication could be taken for what it was worth. Pizza was the sort of fellow that could get away with remarks of that nature. Dorn liked his looks—a man obviously satirizing officers in general, and probably himself most of all. But too subtly for the rest of that vain species to notice it.

"Booze is in the usual place," Sarge said. "Help yourselves. I ain't a bartender, as you gents know by now. It's help yourself or go dry."

There were obviously no teetotalers in the crowd except Dorn, who considered himself on duty. The others took it for granted that a man of his calling had to stay sober to stay alive.

"First jack deals," Sarge stated, shuffling and running the pack of cards he'd just opened. He always kept several dozen sealed new decks, specially ordered from a St. Louis supplier so his guests could be sure he hadn't marked them. The simpletons he always had in his poker sessions were too green to suspect that the supplier Sarge used was privately famous among professional gamblers for his marked sealed decks.

General Dilly got the deal. He took the cards eagerly. "I feel lucky tonight," he exulted. He always felt lucky. Dilly's Luck was a byword in the army. Or as the saying went, "A dumb shit like him had to be lucky to get where he is." His cute wife's flirting and whatever else she did with the top brass hadn't hurt either.

Sarge waited till Dorn's dealing had been able to get General Dilly and Agent Crumm heavily in hock to him. Customarily Sarge kicked back a substantial sum to both of them whenever he sold Crumm a herd. Everyone involved understood that arrangement was to ensure that he stayed exclusive supplier, in the first place, and that General Dilly didn't blow the whistle on the Indian agent for buying "wet" stock in the second. It also softened, and sometimes totally absorbed, the poker losses of two notoriously lousy card players. These facts were the background for Sarge's next remark.

"I hear you bought a herd from someone else the other day," he said to Crumm. "I hope you got the usual commission."

"What's that?" Dilly came to attention. He wasn't dumb where his financial well-being was concerned.

Crumm looked uncomfortable, pretending to study his cards closely as Sarge continued: "Yeah. I guess there's a new supplier, General. Well, that's okay. Business is so good here I don't need the money."

Dilly glared at Crumm. "What the hell's the deal?" he asked bluntly.

Crumm shrugged. "I needed cattle. Sarge didn't have any. My Indians were hungry. Next thing they'd have jumped the reservation after buffalo and likely some of your boys would have got killed chasing them, General." It sounded logical, but his face reddened as he talked.

"You know where those cattle came from?" Sarge asked innocently.

"Up north," Crumm stated. "Over the divide."

"My foot," Sarge said. "They were rustled off my supplier."

"Haw," Major Bulstrode guffawed. Everyone there knew where Sarge's supplier got his cattle in the first place. Major Pizza promptly joined in the general laugh that followed. The situation was so patently ludicrous that even General Dilly could see the humor in it.

"Who sold you them cows?" Sarge asked.

Crumm bridled at his tone. "I don't have to tell you my business."

Sarge got a wicked gleam in his eye. "Maybe you'd like to tell the new deputy sheriff, then." He indicated Dorn with his thumb. Dorn remained impassive, eyeing Crumm woodenly.

"Hell," Crumm burst out. "There's no big secret. I just didn't like the way you were sweating me. I got 'em from a rancher from up around Bozeman named George Chutney."

"Big-Nosed George Chutney?" Sarge asked.

"I don't know about that. Come to think of it, though, he did have a sort of a beak."

"He's the biggest damn rustler in the Northwest," Sarge snorted. He neglected to add what else he was thinking: Next to Cantoon.

"I didn't know that," Crumm said.

"I believe that," Sarge said. "I'll let it slide this once, for old times' sake. But if he shows up again, get word to me or Dorn right away."

"Any chance of running him down?" General Dilly asked. "I can give Dorn a patrol of troops as long as word doesn't get out. Call it a routine scout."

"No chance," Sarge said. "Big-Nosed George is too slick. Be gone till things cool down. He may be in New York seein' the sights by now. Or in his case more likely feelin' 'em."

Before the game ended Crumm had paid for his apostasy in coin of the realm. He was out about six months' pay. "If you're a leetle short," Sarge suggested, "I can take your note and give you back your cash."

It was this sort of generosity with other people's money that made Sarge a general favorite. In fact, generosity was the only difference between him and regular bankers. Both got a return from people for letting them use their own money. And neither was suspected by most of his victims.

When the others were all gone, Sarge winked at Dorn. "Slick as axle grease," he said. "Old Dilly'll be better than Pinkerton's at watching Crumm for us from now on—and he won't be sending us a bill. Let's see, I cleared about eight hundred bucks. You must have dragged at least four hundred. Not bad."

"Which means you owe me about two hundred," Dorn said.

Sarge looked startled. "What the hell for?"

"Fifty-fifty, old pal. Remember?"

Sarge glumly counted out two hundred dollars. "I wish I could get a cardsharp that can't count," he lamented.

"They're like two-bit diamonds."

"How's that?"

"They don't make 'em. I think I'll turn in." By this time Dorn had Hattie on permanent loan to Sarge. Mattie was staying with the O'Neals till the missus was able to get on her feet. Dorn thought, it was a good thing. After all that *talking* with Breck he could barely spit, much less do anything else. In fact he had a hard time dragging himself to bed. His last thought before he corked off was, If I turn over tonight's take to Mrs. O'Neal, I wonder if she'll believe I found part of her husband's bankroll.

Dorn made that his first job in the morning. When he arrived at the O'Neal cottage, he found them all at the breakfast table, even Mrs. O'Neal. She had some color in her cheeks, but still looked weak and tired.

"How can we ever thank you enough?" she asked Dorn as he joined them for a cup of coffee.

The look she gave him was thanks enough. It affected him somewhat like her daughter Annie's innocent big-eyed appraisals, only there was something vastly different in his reaction to Marie. He felt a trifle weak from about the gizzard down. He hadn't noticed before how pretty she was, in an ethereal sort of way. It made him feel like Sir Galahad somehow. Little Annie's big hug and moist kiss from soft, warm little lips didn't hurt his morale either. When she turned him loose it was Abe's turn, and the boy climbed up on his knee. "Horsey," he said, and Dorn bounced him up and down, causing the child to laugh happily. "More," he urged when Dorn stopped.

"No, Abe," his mother said. "You'll tire Mr. Dorn."

"You can call me Bat," Dorn said. "Everyone else does. And I love to bounce him. Wish I had one of my own. And a girl like Annie, too."

He hadn't thought what he was saying, but he noticed the sudden change in Mrs. O'Neal's eyes, as though she was thinking a forbidden thought. He wondered if he'd hurt her by reminding her that she had no man now. To hurt her was the last thing in the world he wanted to do. He was now even more perplexed about how to broach the money business to her. He'd put it in an envelope and cooked up what he considered a plausible lie. Finally he took the bull by the horns.

"I been doing some detective work. Hunted around down where Mr. O'Neal was found. I don't know how it was missed at the time, but I found this under the boardwalk." He handed her the envelope, which he'd carefully smeared around in the dirt. "Good thing it was in an envelope or it might have been blown away."

She looked in the envelope and drew a sudden breath, turning pale.

"I counted it," he said. "It's over six hundred dollars. I'm sorry that someone must have got some of it—but I'll keep on the case. Your husband won over twice that much."

She looked doubtful, as though she might suspect the truth. He gulped, but couldn't think of anything else to say.

"You are an angel," she said. "What did we do to deserve you?"

He found himself blushing. She rose carefully, then came over and kissed his cheek.

Mattie, watching them as she had been between trips to the stove, had sentimental tears in her eyes. She said nothing, but her heart was happy for the O'Neals. She thought, Bat Dorn is a big chief. We're lucky to know him. But at the thought of him being an angel, even she had to suppress a grin.

CHAPTER 11

THE most whimsical personality in Col. Clay Romanza's regiment had been Dr. Elephalet Taliaferro. If he had tried, Dorn probably could have remembered the doctor's observation: "Nothing causes more trouble than a whore who tries to go back to being a virgin."

In view of the doc's calling, Dorn had wondered whether the surgeon had meant that remark in an anatomical or an allegorical sense. Whichever the case, Bat Dorn was about to suffer living proof of Taliaferro's epigram.

The Phoebe was in love. If Dorn had appreciated all aspects of the situation—since he was the object of that love—he would have realized that it was going to be a mixed blessing—in other words, bad news. In a somewhat different, more delicate, sense it was to be bad news for Major Pizza as well. Till the Phoebe's recent fall, the major had been her heartthrob. She loved his curly hair and great soulful eyes. Furthermore, he always kept his toenails trimmed and as a result had never once scarred her ankles or feet in more hectic moments. It was something for which a sensitive lady could be grateful in a business that was usually only monetarily rewarding.

Moreover, she practiced her Italian and French on him, since he was from Savoy where both were used. Pizza was proud of the distinction of being the nephew of that famous son of Savoy, Cavour, the father of Italy. In fact, possibly due to something in the Cavour blood, the fathering instinct had precipitated Pizza's own departure from his native soil. Several imported English fowling pieces and one exquisitely engraved Bavarian scheutzen rifle were kept double charged in his native Savoy by outraged protective papas praying for his return.

The outside rear stairs on the Bilgewater were not, as might have been assumed, a fire escape, at least not in the usual sense. They were a convenience the Phoebe had had installed to spare Major Pizza embarrassment. When he was on fire he frequently went up them. This he did the afternoon of Dorn's fabulous breakfast with Breck.

She answered Pizza's light tap on the door, recognizing his distinctive touch, and braced herself to do what she realized must be done.

"Ah, *ma chérie*," Pizza cried, enveloping her in his huge arms and a cloud of garlic fumes.

Come to think of it, the Phoebe sighed inwardly, the garlic more than offsets the toenails. She was less reluctant, as a result, to do what she had to. She restrained him gently.

"No," she said. "Stop. I've got to talk to you."

"This is no time for talk," he protested, already breathing heavily.

Cupid, never fond of garlic, had retreated to the nearest open window, inhaling gratefully while eyeing Pizza with solemn, unwinking feline eyes. It would have been interesting to know what he was thinking.

"Yes, it is time to talk!" the Phoebe insisted, firmly pushing away the lips that were working on one of her ears.

The major persisted.

"You're eating my ear like a boiled cabbage," she protested, twisting away suddenly.

That got through to Pizza. "What a way to put it," he protested. "You always loved it before."

She regarded him tragically. "That's it," she said. "Before."

He approached again, impulsively, and she dodged away. "What is it?" he asked, alarmed. "Have I done something?"

She was silent a moment, regarding him with great, tragic eyes. "No. No. I've done something."

The thought flashed through Pizza's mind that she'd got a

"dose" from someone. He appreciated her consideration, if that were the problem, in sparing him. The mark of a true lady of good breeding, he thought. He waited, sensing that she had something to get off her mind.

"I'm in love," she finally managed to say. "This isn't right anymore."

He felt himself melting. "You want to get married," he guessed. "Have bambinos."

"Yes," she said.

"But," he protested. "I'm not sure I'd make a good husband. Besides, my profession is dangerous." Also, as he was careful not to mention, he didn't want a wife, especially not a whore, not even one with a lot of money; especially one he thought he could have.

She smiled, almost laughed. "You darling," she said, "I didn't mean you. I'm in love with Bat Dorn. Have been for years."

She didn't notice the stricken look that captured the major's face for a brief instant before his vanity enabled him to carefully mask it. He felt the cold knife cruelly enter his heart and twist. Zounds! How could someone he'd made love to, letting out all the stops, be in love with any but a Pizza? It was inconceivable. He hardly heard her as she explained her past and Dorn's, both of them hopelessly in love since the war and now, almost miraculously, reunited. When her explanations were over, he rose from where he'd slumped on the love seat, stunned, and went to the door glassy-eyed.

"I understand," he said gallantly.

She shook his hand. "You're a real brick," she allowed, using the highest term of praise then in vogue.

As he descended the rear stairs, he was thinking, a real brick? My God! I need a drink!

Life went on as usual in the bustling town of Warbonnet—for everyone except Major Pizza. His romantic soul was not up to a crushing blow of such magnitude. One drink led to another as the days passed into weeks until finally General

Dilly sent the major to the Keeley Institute for the famed cure.

Major Pizza was in deep mourning and also had a terrible case of the snakes. Two of Dilly's trusted old noncoms escorted the major to the Keeley, to feed him and see that he didn't take a drink if offered one by some Good Samaritan, or fall down if he tripped while wearing his straitjacket.

As fate would have it, General Lacey, the Phoebe's father, was currently on one of his protracted visits to the Keeley to try the cure again. As it turned out, Pizza was to be his roommate, a situation that would lead to a good deal of intrigue.

CHAPTER 12

DORN recognized the fellow slipping out the back door of the Bilgewater. In his official position as deputy sheriff, deputy U.S. marshal, and town marshal he had talked with Pinkerton's. The agency had readily sent him a copy of the mug shot that had been taken at the Illinois pen at Joliet when Big-Nosed George Chutney had resided there for a year.

Here's my cattle thief, Dorn thought. Should I nab him or follow him and see what he's up to?

He realized that the chances of making a rustling charge stick when what was rustled had already been stolen once, were seriously slim. Nor was he certain that Indian Agent Jack Crumm could be persuaded to testify against Chutney.

Best follow him, Dorn concluded.

He hated to do it since he'd been bound for the Bilgewater's fire escape on other pressing early-morning business.

Big-Nosed George hot-footed it out of the Bilgewater for the livery stable as though on an urgent mission. Dorn shadowed him carefully, keeping out of sight. He knew that if he could spot so much as one set of the tracks of Chutney's mount he could round up one of the Indian girls and have her trail it. They were both expect trackers, and he was certain they could follow a shod horse to the gates of hell if need be. Accordingly, a short while later he and Mattie were mounted and in pursuit of Big-Nosed George.

Once out of town, the trail cut away from the road, headed for the broken country south of the river. The two pursuers were careful to stay well behind their quarry, out of sight. At one point Mattie led the way up a hill off the trail.

"See if he's still goin'," she explained. "Maybe he watch back-trail and see us."

It was a good precaution. Warily edging to the hill's crest, they peeked over from behind some dwarf pines. They were just in time to see Chutney turn up a draw, tie his mount out of sight, then return to watch his back-trail. Mattie looked questioningly at Dorn. He shrugged. "We'll wait him out. When he's sure no one is following, he'll go on."

He sat down and rolled them both cigarettes. Mattie puffed contentedly, the picture of one at peace with herself and her world, wishing to be no other place and doing no other thing. Dorn had no complaints about her other than her overfondness for Mrs. Hawley's Vegetable Compound and also Hostettler's Anaconda Appetite Bitters, both of which were about 50 percent pure alcohol. He wished she would stick to Anheuser-Busch's less potent bottled goods.

He had rolled them two more cigarettes before they got some action. It wasn't what he'd expected, however. A second rider came on Chutney's trail, galloping hard, raising a cloud of dust. Dorn looked to see if Chutney would raise his rifle to pot-shoot whoever it was. If he did, Dorn intended to fire a shot first and warn the second rider, regardless of who it might be. It wasn't necessary. Chutney hadn't been watching his back-trail; he'd been waiting for this individual. All Dorn could make out at that distance even with his field glass was that the new rider wore a long linen duster and a large-brimmed black hat.

The two riders soon set out together at a lope. Once they were out of sight, Dorn led the way directly down to their trail. At each ridge he and Mattie took the same precaution, circling away from the trail to avoid being observed. By then the sun was high and hot, bringing out the sweat on both horses and riders. Dorn suspected they were about to have the purpose of these two mysterious riders revealed to them when he heard the distant bawling of a herd of cattle. He and Mattie tied their mounts and this time *very* cautiously snaked to the crest of the hill before them. Their path brought them to a caprock of large limestone slabs. Some hundred yards below they could see their quarry standing now with several other men who had obviously been awaiting their coming. In the distance, on the far side of the canyon, was a herd of longhorns, retained in a tributary box canyon by a rude brush fence.

Dorn grinned, suspecting that old Cantoon was about to lose another herd. He'd have bet that Sarge Hoak's rustler and his boys were sleeping one off back in town, probably in the hayloft of the livery stable. If they are, he told himself, it's a pity I didn't know it. He'd have loved to witness the West's two premier rustlers in an eyeball-to-eyeball confrontation. He thought of sending Mattie back to town for Cantoon, but concluded it was too far and would take too long.

"We'll see what they do," he told Mattie, "as if we can't guess."

"They'll steal them critters," Mattie assured him.

"Yup. That's my guess. And if they do, we'll tag along and see where they take 'em."

As much hell as General Dilly had raised with Crumm, he'd bet they didn't try to market another herd at Fort Littleworth.

Cantoon hadn't expected anyone to have the gall to lift a second herd from him, one would guess. He probably hadn't expected Big-Nosed George to have the guts to come back so soon.

"Hey," Mattie whispered, grasping Dorn's shirtsleeve. "Look there." She pointed. "Them two are the little braves you kick ass on plenty."

Dorn squinted, but he couldn't be sure, except to make out that two of those below were Indians. However, he had learned long before to implicitly trust an Indian's eyes. He'd known them to spot antelope and tell their number farther away than he could see the animals with his naked eye, a fact he'd then confirmed with a powerful field glass.

"Yup," she stated positively. "Them're Badger's Navel and Sitting Rat." Indians were often named for the first thing their mother saw or thought of after their birth. Later, as warriors, they often took other names—not too surprisingly.

Dorn had been doing some thinking about the purposeful way Chutney had exited the Bilgewater, got his horse, and ridden out here. He recalled that the first herd of cattle had been rustled—in effect from Sarge Hoak—as soon as Fancy Venere had learned that Sarge was building a joint to compete with the Bilgewater. It figured that the rider who'd come hightailing out to join Chutney was Fancy Venere himself. *I give him higher marks for guts than I figured he deserved,* Dorn told himself. *I had him slotted for the kind of hairpin that'd hire his dirty work done.* His train of thought returned to the scene below. Just maybe, he reasoned, Cantoon left a guard or two behind.

The group below moved confidently toward the box-canyon corral. *Those Injuns likely spied the place out,* he thought. Assuming that, he was in for a huge surprise. Chutney personally opened the corral gate and started to circle the cattle, followed by the others. In a short while they had the herd of some two hundred beeves lined out eastward.

Mattie was the first to spot the stream of riders scrambling from the opposite tree line, pistols drawn. "Look, Dorn," she said.

He recognized Cantoon in the lead, spurring his mount forward, six-shooter held high until within shooting range. One of Cantoon's men started firing a trifle early and disclosed their presence.

Chutney rapidly gave his crew orders, part starting the cattle into a run, and a half-dozen others moving to stand off Cantoon's attack. Dorn was amazed to see Fancy Venere unlimber a double-barreled shotgun from a thong on his saddlehorn and charge directly at Cantoon. The first barrel must have come uncomfortably close to Cantoon, who sheered away, spurring as rapidly to get out of range as he had to get in range. Taking their cue from him, his boys broke off the attack. They collectively got the second barrel as they retreated, Venere clinging hot on their trail, guiding his horse with his knees in a display of horsemanship a cossack would have been proud of. He reloaded as he came, losing his hat from the rushing air at that breakneck pace. Within moments, Cantoon and his men were out of sight.

Dorn's mouth involuntarily dropped open as he saw long yellow hair stream out that had previously been tucked up under the hat. My God, he thought. It's the Boy General, it ain't Venere. That could only be one of Dilly's famous go-to-hell charges. What the hell's he doing rustling cows? Then he remembered those gambling debts.

The distant rider broke off pursuit and trotted back, regaining the black hat, but letting the long hair remain out now that it had been revealed anyhow. "I didn't think that was Fancy Venere's style," Dorn said half aloud.

"General Dilly," he said to Mattie, pointing. He didn't notice her puzzled look but would recall it later, as well as the fact that she seemed about to say something but withheld the remark.

Dorn and Mattie surreptitiously trailed the herd at a distance, keeping always well out of sight. In midafternoon General Dilly broke off and headed back toward Fort Littleworth alone. Dorn considered going back to round up Cantoon and his boys, but he decided they'd had too much fight taken out of them to be worth much in another try to recover the cattle.

Chutney pushed the rustled stock hard that day, ending up at nightfall some twenty-five miles away from where he'd started, Dorn and Mattie following all the way. They made camp a couple of miles from the herd, masking a small fire for their coffee and bacon in a cave Mattie found up under a caprock cliff. She found a bunch of absolutely dry wood so no smoke would reveal their position.

Dorn watched her work, admiring her efficiency. He said, "I can't get over how you Injuns can set a fire that never smokes."

Mattie grinned. "Not always. You want 'em never to smoke, you know the only way to do?"

He shook his head, waiting for a priceless revelation of Indian lore and got it.

"Don't light 'em."

She laughed a long while over her joke. At first he was too stunned at this unexpected sense of humor in a stolid Indian to have the wit to join her. Then he laughed too.

"Damned if that ain't true," he agreed, still grinning. He could hardly wait to catch Sarge Hoak on that one.

Nights got cold even in midsummer in that country, but Mattie made them a warm bed of their four blankets, including saddle blankets, in which they slept curled snugly together. They turned in unison, in the army fashion that Dorn recalled all too well. In a crowded army tent the men had to sleep like closely packed spoons in a drawer. One man would yell, "Spoon," and they'd all turn together by a subconscious reflex that was soon acquired. It was the same with him and Mattie. He started to mention it to her when he realized she was already snoring.

Dorn was awakened by the appetizing smell of coffee brewing and bacon cooking. He rolled out and wandered away to relieve himself politely out of sight. He was ruminating on a proper course of action. Somehow he had to put a stop to the drain on Hoak's rustled cattle, since that was, in a real sense, also his bread and butter. He was considering the matter as he went over to the fire. He guessed that Chutney was probably aiming to drive the rustled herd over into Dakota—probably peddle them at one of the Sioux agencies over there.

"I wish I knew how we could get our hands on that herd," he observed idly.

Mattie gave him a surprised look, as though she couldn't believe her ears. "You want them cows?" she asked, to make sure she'd heard him right.

"Hell yes," he told her. "Why did you think we're followin' 'em?"

She shrugged. "Damfino."

"Well," he said. "Unless I can find us a couple of more men to help drive 'em, we might as well forget it."

"No big deal," Mattie said. "Wait'll tonight."

He eyed her suspiciously. "What do you aim to do, get yourself killed?"

"No chance," she snorted. "Go down and do some thumb-whistling."

"What the hell is thumb-whistling?"

She showed him, cupping her hands and placing the thumbs side by side and blowing into a small space between them. While doing this, she uncupped her hands, then recupped them alternately. The result was a good imitation of an owl's hoot.

"Thumb-whistling," she said.

"I see. Then what happens?"

"Badger's Navel and Sitting Rat hear um and come."

He eyed her skeptically. "What then?"

"We hire 'em."

"And what do we pay 'em?"

She grinned. "You wanna give 'em back some ponies or them Winchesters?"

He thought it over. It was a pretty high price to pay for raking Sarge's chestnuts. He knew Hoak wouldn't be anxious to repay him.

"Not really," he answered her honestly.

"Hokay," she said, still grinning. "Lots of stuff braves need they can't carry along on the warpath. You let me dicker with them two. Maybe I got something they want."

A bright little lamp went on in his head suddenly. He

considered the sacredness of his relationship to Mattie and Hattie. Then he considered the value of good horses and Winchesters. Thrift overcame scruples.

"Okay," he agreed. "You hire Badger's Navel and Sitting Rat. Bring 'em in and I'll take it from there."

The hiring worked out just as Mattie had promised. In addition to the two young braves, she brought in most of Chutney's rations that she'd told them to steal.

Just as the moon went down, Dorn's cowboys struck, yelling and waving blankets. The longhorns leaped to their feet, lurching into motion as soon as they were up. Chutney's crew fired a few futile shots before the herd trampled over their camp, running like startled deer. They left behind a thoroughly shaken and demoralized band of rustlers, afoot as well, since Dorn had directed the stampede where it would probably sweep away their horses, which it did.

Those fools shoulda left a night guard at least, he thought. I hope old Chutney didn't get stomped to death. He sort of liked Chutney's style. He liked General Dilly's style even better. The Army of the Northern Virginia had had a grudging admiration for the Boy General, even if he was a blue-bellied damn-Yankee and consequently an obviously no-good, spoon-stealing son of a bitch.

Dorn grinned, remembering. As one of Mosby's Rangers, he'd spent a good deal of time trying to dry-gulch or kidnap Dilly. But, for all of his posing, the Boy General was obviously a fighter.

Dorn found the two Indian bucks such good cowboys he almost lost his head and gave them back their Winchesters when they got the herd back to Warbonnet. Instead, he gave them a can of beans apiece when Sarge wasn't looking.

Dorn debated telling Sarge that Dilly was probably behind the recent rustlings, but a familiar inner voice cautioned him: Not yet. He always heeded that voice. Not that he had the slightest intention of double-crossing his partner. It'll wait, Dorn told himself. First I've gotta figure out a way to sound Dilly out about what the hell he thinks he's doing.

CHAPTER 13

FATE had granted the construction foreman of the Sioux Falls, Yankton and Fort Littleworth Railroad a truly appropriate name—O'Phender. He'd already been in jail twice in each of the first two towns in the railroad's name, and in the guardhouse at Fort Littleworth once, all inside of a year, during which construction had been in progress on the last few hundred miles of the line into Warbonnet. The charge in each case had been drinking and fighting. It had taken a platoon of soldiers to get him into the Fort Littleworth guardhouse. At Sioux Falls, which was becoming civilized and effete, the local militia company had been mobilized both times to arrest him. He'd crippled the captain, a sergeant, and three privates before landing behind bars the first time. The second, they cowed him with a cannon full of nails. Yankton, like Warbonnet, still had a frontier-style marshal, Whang Leather Smith, who had simply tiptoed up behind the drunken Irishman and dropped him with a dexterously applied blow from a pick handle both times. He'd then drafted some riverboat roustabouts to carry the massive inert form to the jail.

When it became known that this formidable Irishman was on his way to Bat Dorn's bailiwick, a reasonable amount of interest was generated over the possibility of a bare-knuckle bout between the two and, naturally, in the outcome, if one should occur. Wager boards sprang into existence on the matter in all the saloons, discreetly kept out of sight under the bar with the night sticks, brass knuckles, and Bulldog five-shooters that every prudent bartender kept as appurtenances for survival. The boards were kept from sight out of deference to the sensibilities of the town marshal, since the odds ran heavily in favor of the railroader; after all, he outweighed Bat by a good hundred pounds and had a mighty impressive record. Besides, he was a blusterer, like Yahoo Dave Storms, which scared a good many people. By contrast everyone knew that Dorn smiled a lot and laughed often. Of course there was his cold look, reserved for barroom entrances, but almost the whole community had figured out that he donned that as a matter of protocol—more or less to keep from offending the rest of the star-toting fraternity in case they heard he'd been seen smiling. It was universally understood and forgiven.

Perhaps Warbonnet's one denizen who was happiest over the prospect of a possible showdown between Dorn and O'Phender was Fancy Venere. He had a plan. It was based on his estimate of Sarge Hoak's probably blind loyalty to his old buddy Dorn. In fact, Venere had started the first wager board in town. Nor was he satisfied with the notion of a fight being merely prospective. He made sure that word reached O'Phender from time to time regarding what Warbonnet figured Dorn could do to him. After he allowed that had had a proper effect, he made sure that O'Phender heard what Dorn himself allegedly had said he'd do to him. That was all it took. Without further effort by Venere, word began to drift into Warbonnet about what O'Phender planned to do to Warbonnet, and its marshal if he tried to interfere, as soon as his Irish lordship could work a trip there into his busy schedule. Several citizens, no doubt injured in the vicinity of their civic pride, dutifully rushed the news to Dorn.

About the best they could get out of the marshal was a mild, unperturbed "Do tell?" Dorn was beginning to get the hang of one important aspect of his job. Threats. They were best ignored. Learning to do that was one of the most difficult aspects of a frontier marshal's job. Those who survived did—perhaps their thick skins were one reason they were hard to down.

Dorn had started a regular practice of having morning coffee at the O'Neal cottage around seven. By now he was on a first-name basis with Marie, who was up and quite strong, though Mattie or Hattie still came in sometimes to help.

"You ought to eat something solid for breakfast," Marie O'Neal cautioned him. "You can't live on coffee."

"It'd be supper if I did," he said. "I'm usually up all night. Fact is, I'm goin' over to bed right after I leave here."

Marie smiled. "I should have known that. Mr. O'Neal kept about the same kind of hours. Why don't you let me fix you supper, then?"

He didn't see any tactful way to tell her he'd had "supper" and dessert down at the Bilgewater a couple of hours earlier. "How about 'breakfast' this evenin' when I go on shift?" he suggested.

"You've got a deal," Marie said. It was a phrase she'd picked up from her late husband.

Dorn was pleased with her improvement. He'd hoped she would go back to her folks in Illinois, but she seemed inclined to stay in Warbonnet. He wouldn't have believed her reason if anyone but she had told him, and she wasn't about to. He should have suspected from the way she looked at him, but he, like most men—despite his considerable experience with women—was almost a complete dunce where they were concerned.

Dorn hadn't been able to analyze his feelings toward Marie O'Neal. He knew they were vastly different from what he felt toward the Phoebe. He rightly felt he was in love with Breck, knew he had been for years, and her calling made absolutely no difference to him. Besides, she was now exclusively his, he assumed, except for a need to be tactful to Fancy Venere for old times' sake, which Dorn reluctantly accepted. Neither of them mentioned it. But when he looked at Marie, his feeling was entirely different. There was an element of both respect and worship involved, also a pure sort of love like that evoked by little Annie, with her wistful eyes and warm, loving little hugs and kisses.

Dorn suspected that he was also falling in love with Marie, but in an entirely different, "wholesome" way. The notion of any physical sort of relationship with Marie had never entered Dorn's head. This was something she recognized but scarcely appreciated. If he had known what her plans for him were, he wouldn't have believed them either. He was blissfully unaware, as well, what her profession had been when Square Deal O'Neal had taken her away from it. He may have suspected if he'd thought about it, but would have rejected the idea as too ridiculous. Nonetheless, professional gamblers didn't have an opportunity to meet many respectable women on the frontier. Neither did lawmen, as Dorn's case proved. But he was happy with the women he met—a point to ponder.

Marie was sitting across the oilcloth-covered kitchen table from Dorn. The children had gone out to play. Without preamble she asked, "Have you ever heard of a railroad man named O'Phender?"

Dorn appraised her speculatively. He could imagine what was on her mind, showing how widespread was the local anticipation of a possible battle royal soon.

"Happens I have," he said. "Why do you ask?" He sipped his coffee, eyes still on her face.

She looked frightened. "He means you some harm. The word is all over town. Haven't you heard?"

He laughed. "Shore have. The whole town made sure of that. Got tote boards in every saloon keepin' track of the betting."

"Aren't you worried? What do you plan to do? I've seen him. He's a giant."

"Well," Dorn said, "let's hope the old sayin' is true: 'The bigger they are the harder they fall.'" He laughed at a sudden thought. "Maybe I can get him in range of that singletree I used on old Cantoon."

"I hope so," she said. "I'll be glad when they get the new marshal and you go to running Sarge's new place."

By then Sarge's imposing new joint was almost finished. If

the interior fixtures hadn't been temporarily stranded on the way up the Missouri on a steamer that had grounded on a sandbar, the grand opening would have occurred already.

Dorn was touched by her concern. He reached out impulsively and took her hand in his. "Don't worry about old Bat Dorn. He can take care of himself." The thought passed through his mind that at least his legs were in good working order, and his stomach muscles were as hard as steel.

He noticed the look on her face for the first time, as he held her hand. The dark eyes were now wide and pure black. She was breathing swiftly. He started to blush and rose suddenly.

"Well, I reckon I'd better be goin'," he gulped.

She was in his path, small and determined. He wasn't sure how they started to kiss, but he was sure, very shortly, that she was no amateur at it. With her body she quickly conveyed the depth of her need for him, though he could scarcely believe what he had to believe. He drew back to look at her and catch his breath. She insistently pulled him close again. After another deep kiss she said, "I'll send Annie and Abe after some berries."

Dorn couldn't think of a single thing to say to that. In fact, it made excellent sense to him under the circumstances.

An hour or so later as he dragged slowly upstairs at Sarge's, he was thinking, What the hell do you know about this? He was damn glad neither of his Injun wives was around. He fell asleep almost as soon as his head hit the pillow.

Downstairs a transaction was taking place that would have disturbed him, in fact, would—mightily—as soon as he found out about it. Sarge had been alone in the store when Fancy Venere stolled in—a circumstance that Venere had tried to be sure of. Sarge noted his entrance.

"Well, well," he greeted Venere. "A real honor. What can I do for your grace?"

Venere grinned amiably, a dangerous sign. "No sense in

beatin' around the bush. I got a proposition for a gamblin' man like you."

"I ain't interested," Sarge said at once.

"I think you will be, especially if word gets around you ain't got the courage of your convictions."

"What the hell're you talkin' about?"

Sarge prided himself on his guts. He was also the type that worried about his reputation, as Venere had divined. That "if word gets around" was the kind of threat that bothered him. Venere watched him, suspecting that his jibe had hit home.

"Well?" Venere said. "You got the guts to back your own man or not?"

"Meanin' what?" Sarge asked.

"The odds are about two to one that O'Phender will kick Bat Dorn up the street and out of town. What do you say to that?"

"Bull! I've seen Dorn fight."

"I've seen O'Phender fight, too. All Dorn's done is deck a couple of drunk freighters."

"It don't signify," Sarge said. "You'll see."

"Yeah I will. I hear O'Phender'll hit town tonight. So here's my proposition. I've already spread it around town I'm down here to make it. This town ain't big enough for the two of us. I'll bet you my new store and the Bilgewater against this place and your new dive that O'Phender kicks the shit out of Dorn—and on top of that whichever one of us loses the bet leaves town."

"You must think I'm crazy," Sarge said. "That big baboon might get lucky."

Venere sneered. "That's what I figured. The boys said you wouldn't put your money where your mouth is."

"Who the hell said that?"

"Everybody."

"Okay," Sarge said grimly, not liking it a bit. "You got a deal." He stuck his big paw out and had the satisfaction of making Venere wince as he crushed down on the French-man's limp hand. "You want it in writing?" Sarge asked.

"Nope," Venere said, "your word's good with me."

Sarge was so pleased with the thought that he forgot to ask himself if Venere's word was good with him, until later. When he did, he said to himself, The hell with it. Dorn ain't gonna lose no fight anyhow. Then he added, At least I sure as hell hope not. I'm too damn old to start over. He cursed himself inwardly for being sucked into a risky gamble by an appeal to his pride. What a damn fool pickle to get myself into, he thought. Suppose the big faker does lose. He groaned.

All of these circumstances soon became known to the Phoebe, who was first and foremost a hardheaded business-woman. If she hadn't been she wouldn't have survived her postwar adversity. She certainly didn't want to see Dorn hurt by O'Phender. On the other hand, she didn't want to see the Bilgewater lost. Fortunately she'd known O'Phender at other times in other places. He roared and he sashayed and swashbuckled when in his cups, but he was a man with a shrewd love for a dollar above all. She planned to have a business conference with him before any rough stuff started. Accordingly she sent an emissary to make sure that he came to Warbonnet just after dark and made his way up the fire escape to her suite before he had his first drink—other than the usual fuel from a pocket flask, of course, which any sane man carried.

This transpired while Dorn slept. He arose after dark, recalling his "breakfast" appointment at Marie O'Neal's. The thought of the sweet, demure little mother and their morn-ing transaction introduced complete confusion into his mind. Could that really have happened, he asked himself, or did I dream it? He was convinced it hadn't been a dream. If it had, it was the kind a man needed more of. He thought of

Annie and Abe and how he'd wished he could have a pair of his own kids like them. The whole thing forced him to reassess his relationship with the Phoebe. He was almost sure Breck wasn't the marrying kind in the first place. In the second, he was sure she wasn't the family type, assuming she was still young enough to have kids. He was pretty sure he couldn't talk either the Phoebe or Marie into signing up to join his existing sacred arrangement with Mattie and Hattie.

"What a mess," he said.

Sarge wandered in, having heard Dorn stirring around and having overheard his remark. "What mess is that?" he asked.

"Women," Dorn said. "Too many of 'em."

"Beats too few from what I've seen," Sarge allowed. "Besides, the gals all like you."

"I know," Dorn said. "I know."

"So?"

"You wouldn't believe me if I told you."

"Try me."

"Nope," Dorn said. "At least not yet. I ain't the kiss-and-tell type."

Sarge snorted. "Now who the hell's drawers have you been in?"

Dorn merely grinned.

"Well, the hell with women," Sarge said. "That ain't what I came to talk about. We got a bigger problem."

Dorn looked expectantly at his friend. "We?"

"We. Us. You 'n' me." He told Dorn about his bet with Fancy Venere.

Dorn gave him a disgusted look. "You idjit!" he exploded. "Suppose the big baboon gets in a lucky punch?"

"I thought o' that," Sarge said.

"Well, you should o' thought of it a helluva lot sooner."

"You could skip out," Sarge suggested, not hopefully.

"Bat Dorn doesn't run."

"Horseshit."

"I've got some other responsibilities."

"The Phoebe?"

Dorn nodded. "That ain't all. There's the two O'Neal kids. They need a paw."

"Marie'll find a man. She's a good-lookin' filly. In fact I may go over there in the mornin' and take her a bunch of posies."

The idea didn't sit too well with Dorn—of Sarge or any other man going over there. He slyly taunted Sarge, "Better wait'll O'Phender blows in. You may not have very good prospects for supporting a wife after the big brawl."

Sarge winced. "I better have."

"I've whipped bigger'n him," Dorn said. Sarge looked brighter. "On the other hand," Dorn added, "I've been whipped by littler than me." Sarge looked glummer.

They were interrupted by the arrival of Cantoon. He was comparatively sober and had been ever since Dorn had hired him as assistant marshal.

"O'Phender's down at the Bilgewater," he announced. "He ain't broke nothin' yet. You want I should just save us all a lot of trouble and kill him sorta permanent?" He looked hopeful. So did Sarge.

"Naw," Dorn said. "I'll be down in a while and give him his chance. Let him spread and blow."

Dorn carefully washed and shaved, put on a clean shirt and his lefty gunfighter rig, his business pistol in his right back pocket. He donned a coat. looked at himself in the mirror, and strolled out whistling softly. He reflected that whistling might not be so easy to do for the next few days. It was hard to manage through a split lip.

"You're later than I expected," Marie greeted him. "The kids are in bed." She looked hopeful.

"I can't have breakfast," he explained.

She looked disappointed.

"Business," he said. "O'Phender's in town. Down at the Bilgewater."

She came near and put her arms around him. "Do you have to go down and meet him? I don't want you hurt."

He held her at arm's length, looking into her lovely, concerned eyes. "I'm afraid so," he said. "It's the Code of the West."

"I know," she said in a low voice. "It stinks."

He looked surprised for a moment. "Come to think of it, you're dead right," he agreed. "But there's a lot more than honor ridin' on this bout."

"What?" she asked.

He told her about Sarge's bet.

"The idiot!" she said.

He looked even more surprised. He was rapidly discovering there was more to Marie O'Neal than he'd suspected—or bargained for.

"Wish me luck," he said.

"I'll do better'n that," she said. She left for a moment and returned with a stout pick handle. "This is what Whang Leather Smith over at Yankton used on him," she said.

"How'd you hear that?"

"The newspaper."

He took it and hefted it. When he left, he was carrying it inconspicuously at his side. At the Bilgewater he deposited it outside, out of sight behind a rain barrel at one corner.

Then he stepped up to the batwings, adjusted his hat, and pushed them open, stepping through and letting them swing to behind him. He was wearing his best "dramatic entrance" poker face, eyes slitted. He spotted the towering bulk of O'Phender at the bar, a clear space for several feet on each side of him. There could be no mistaking his man. The giant turned, suspecting from the sudden hush who had arrived. This was an old, familiar game to him. He glowered at Dorn from under a black slouch hat, holding a shot glass in one hand, eyes glittering evilly.

Dorn crossed to the bar, standing half facing him. "Mr. O'Phender, I presume," he said.

"Yah," the other growled. "Big Harry O'Phender. You got any objections?"

"I hear you're gonna tear my asshole out."

"You hear right." He moved toward Dorn.

"You want I should kill the son of a bitch now?" Cantoon called hopefully from the end of the bar.

O'Phender stopped, slowly turned toward the voice. He swung back to Dorn. "Whipsawed, by gawd," he said. "I thought you had guts enough to have this out man to man. I ain't no gunslinger."

"Take it easy, Cantoon," Dorn ordered. "Just make sure this outgrown jasper doesn't jump me while I shuck my coat and shootin' irons."

There was a deathly silence in the Bilgewater as Dorn stripped down to fight. Discreetly hidden by the shadows at the top of the stairs the Phoebe watched.

CHAPTER 14

THE inner pocket of the coat Dorn laid on the bar before his skirmish with Big Harry O'Phender contained a highly interesting note. The notepaper was delicately perfumed. The fluted edge of this fancy paper had flicked into sight as Dorn folded his coat, taking his thoughts briefly off his impending battle. For a few seconds his mind was only dimly concerned with his surroundings. He was barely aware that a new flock of eager, noisy observers was converging on the Bilgewater, the word passing rapidly up the street that Dorn had appeared. Many had rushed away from partially consumed suppers. In his temporary preoccupation, Dorn almost missed detecting O'Phender's first clumsy roundhouse swing on its way. But not quite. He neatly ducked under it and retaliated with the old one-two. One was to the gut, spilling the breath out of his huge opponent; two was to the jaw, spinning O'Phender to the floor, where he sat stunned, flat on the seat of his tentlike trousers. He shook his head in foggy bewilderment. He'd never faced a pro before. Dimly he heard the excited shout that had gone up, almost involuntarily, from a crowd that had hardly expected this result at all, much less so soon.

Dorn's mind was still perilously distracted. He scarcely heard someone's savage cry, "Give him the boots, Dorn." What was distracting him was the realization that he hadn't had time to respond to the request in that perfumed note. It troubled him a great deal as a matter of fact, but he had a good reason for not having answered it.

He'd come by the note after a series of incidents that had started out innocently enough a few days before. Most of his woman trouble began that way. He hadn't been able to think up a subterfuge by which to approach General Dilly about his complicity in cattle rustling, so he had decided to take the bull by the horns and drop in on him as deputy U.S. marshal on official business. Dorn's own unsupported testimony would not have been enough to convict the flamboyant cavalryman. He realized also that because she was an Indian Mattie's word in a white court wouldn't have been accepted if she testified that water was usually wet. So Dorn had planned to generally discuss the matter of rustling and the general's prior offer of troops as a posse commitatus to see what might come out of the officer on that subject. Dorn assumed that Dilly would naturally be reluctant to assign troops that might inadvertently bag their own commander. In such an event, the general had a legitimate cover, of course; the use of troops in such matters was now illegal, but that hadn't discouraged the general earlier from making a similar offer, proposing to use the subterfuge of calling them a "routine patrol."

When Dorn arrived at Fort Littleworth, however, the general hadn't been in his office. An orderly had suggested that Dorn try the commanding officer's house, which he pointed out to him across the parade ground. Dorn had led his horse partway across the parade ground when he was accosted by a two-man guard detail with rifles held at high port, barring his way.

"Halt!" one of them cried. He halted, amused at their officially ferocious facial expressions. Several years in the military had acquainted him with the fact that even unfettered American minds readily fell afoul of the army's unthinking indoctrination in various fatheaded procedures.

"What's the problem?" he asked mildly.

"Didn't you see that Keep Off the Grass sign?"

Dorn looked around, perplexed. He still couldn't see one, or any grass either. "Uh-uh," he admitted.

The sentry pointed to a distant sign, almost invisible at the end of the parade ground, fumbling his rifle as he did and almost dropping it.

Dorn snorted.

The sentry who was doing the talking scowled. "Don't get smart," he snapped.

Dorn was still grinning. "Listen," he said, "if I was smart I wouldn't come within miles of a fort."

The second sentry snorted. His companion gave him a poisonous look. To Dorn he said, "I oughta run you in to the guardhouse."

"Come on," Dorn protested reasonably, "you fellers traipse a few hundred hosses over this ground every night at retreat parade. Why should anyone have to keep off the grass? Besides, there ain't any grass. Any fool can see that. Nary a blade."

It made a lot of sense, which was probably why it stunned the more officious sentry. He looked mulish but rightly concluded he wasn't going to garner any military honors by pursuing the subject. "All the same," he insisted, "yer gonna have to go around."

"Okay, sport," Dorn agreed. He mounted Old Paint, who just then decorated the grassless parade ground. Dorn guffawed and gave the sentry a mock salute. "Maybe that'll help get some grass started," he observed, spinning his horse and spurring him away as Old Paint made one last parting gesture, which rolled to a halt at the sentry's foot. His partner guffawed. "Shut up!" the spokesman suggested.

His partner thought, but wisely forbore to say, I'm glad I'm not buckin' for corporal. He'd rather have had a decent meal—or a woman, decent or not, preferably not, since decent ones were scared to wiggle for fear someone would think they were immoral. He idly watched Dorn's progress around the parade ground and saw him stop at General Dilly's quarters and tie his horse to the fancy wrought-iron hitching post. "Lookee there," he said to his partner. "You just done mouthed off to what's likely a friend of the gin'ral."

He relished watching the other's dismayed expression. Everyone knew Dilly's style; if a meteor had hit his home, he'd have blamed it on the nearest subordinate—admittedly with a fine impartiality for whether it was an officer or enlisted man, which nonetheless garnered him few admirers except among newsmen. Significantly they were not under his jurisdiction.

Dorn admired the general's imposing house with its dozen or so chimneys. Jeez, he thought, there must be a fireplace in every room. If he had added, or a German heater, he'd have been correct. The general's little turtledove, as he called her, was a freezer. In this northern climate, facetiously described by the inhabitants as having just two seasons—winter and the Fourth of July—a freezer had a problem. But not if Dilly and slave labor could avert it. The fort had been built by soldier labor under Dilly's supervision. In cold weather a platoon was kept busy stoking the general's stoves and fireplaces day and night. They'd burned down his former quarters that way, this being his second.

The little turtledove had been home alone and had finally answered Dorn's ring. She'd first appraised him carefully through the bow window from behind heavy lace curtains. What she had seen pleased her, just as it had pleased the Phoebe and Marie O'Neal. If his appearance had not pleased her, she very likely would not have answered the door. But in this case she was secretly glad that the general was out coursing his hounds and that Lottie, her black maid and cook, was shopping. Lately she had frequently felt an uncomfortable irritability around her dashing consort as well as around familiar people generally. She was frequently bored and vaguely distressed in a manner that defied her understanding. Just before Dorn's arrival she had been restlessly pacing the rooms, picking things up, ostensibly examining them but with unseeing eyes, then—frequently—banging them down, especially the photo of General Dilly wearing his first star, looking somehow like a youthful Mars in his self-designed uniform and, contradictorily, somehow like an embarrassed boy trying to ignore his adolescent pimples behind a casual air—and a precocious flowing mustache.

The turtledove who answered Dorn's twisting of the brass doorbell key was many things: deliberately demure, petite, delicately lovely, and happy to see a new, handsome man. She hoped these didn't show too obviously on her face.

"Yes," she enunciated, the one word almost a question as she held the door only partly open, concealing half of her body behind it, though its surface was only of a beveled glass pane. Nonetheless, it muted her form due to a lace curtain stretched over it.

Dorn had heard of this famed beauty whom Dilly had courted and won at the height of the war, having ridden undaunted after her like one of his fabled cavalry charges, across a field roughened by rampant parental objections. She had thereafter followed the general, staying as close to the front lines as circumstances permitted. Dorn almost guffawed when he realized who this winsome lady who answered the door must be. The reason had roots in the distant past. As a member of Mosby's Rangers, Dorn had once captured all her underwear from one of General Dilly's wagons—and also the general's private papers, including a bundle of their love letters. The guffaws around Mosby's campfires hadn't been politely stifled as the Rangers read of the general's "little dirl," as he sometimes addressed her in his love letters.

When Colonel Mosby himself had been apprised of that fact, he had to see one of the letters before he'd believe it. "Well, I do declare," he'd said mildly, once convinced. "You never know." Then he'd remembered his manners. "As gentlemen we must return these things to the general and his lady." Then had added, "After we read all the letters, of course." He'd grinned boyishly, musing again, "I do declare." His brows had suddenly knitted fiercely at another thought, "But it don't signify. We're still gonna kill that blue-bellied

Yankee son of a bitch Dilly if we get the chance." The private material had all been courteously sent back through the lines to General Dilly, except one pair of frilly pantaloons that a private with an underwear fetish hadn't been able to part with. (This had not been generally known, naturally. His Victorian compatriots might have insisted he return it—or at least lend it to them occasionally.)

All this had flitted out of Dorn's memory while he collected himself to say something, since Persephone, Dilly's still impressive wife, had almost taken away his breath. He managed to say, "I'm Marshal Dorn, ma'am."

Her eyes opened a trifle wider. She'd heard of the formidable Bat Dorn. Like most women, especially army women, she was apt to be impressed with a reputation whether it was based on merit or not, which it often wasn't, as in the case of Dorn's—which at least was not rooted in the sort of merit everyone assumed it was.

"Come in," she invited, opening the door wide and gracefully stepping back. She was a diminutive woman, he noted, but not unimpressive. She was sculpted perfection, like a porcelain doll from the hand of a master, pale yet glowing as though from a delicate illumination inside. Her eyes were large and dark, fringed with abundant long lashes. Just then they revealed a faint humorous gleam, as though perhaps recognizing his discomfiture at this unexpected encounter.

"I come—uh, came—to see the general," he blurted.

"He's stepped out for a moment," she replied smoothly. Her eyes never wavered, although she had no idea when the resident swashbuckler might return. "Come in and wait. I'm sure he'll be back soon." The fact was she didn't care if he ever came back, and hadn't for years. She stayed with the general as a matter of financial convenience since her parents had died in debt and had left her no money. This had been almost as big a disappointment to her as it had been to the general, although it hadn't been exactly unexpected.

She led Dorn into the sitting room. "Make yourself at

home," she invited. "I'll fix us some coffee." She hadn't asked if he'd like some, nor had she suggested tea. She'd been on the frontier long enough to know everyone drank coffee. She glanced back suddenly and caught him ogling the dainty sway of her hips accentuated by a bustle. She was smiling as she turned her head quickly away again. "I've got some fritters, too," she called back from somewhere down a hall.

I'll bet that ain't all, either, Dorn thought. He'd already ogled her breasts, pushed high up behind a barely opaque bodice that clung to them and revealed their lithe swaying, pressing insistently like two independent little animals trying to escape from under a blanket. At least that was how they'd impressed Dorn, who would have been glad to do all he could to help them get out. The notion hadn't yet occurred to him that she might invite him to do so. She was far too much a lady in his opinion.

She rolled the coffee and fritters in on a rubber-tired tea cart laid out with immaculate linen and expensive silver and china. He thought this was a trifle ludicrous, since he was dusty, booted, spurred, and wearing two six-shooters. She seemed to sense his unease and the reason for it.

"I'm sorry," she said. "Come out here and you can wash up." She led the way to the kitchen, then left him.

When he returned, she had coffee poured and was pretending to be immersed in a book. He had unbelted his pistols and slung the belts over his arm. She took them and casually hung them next to a saber on a bentwood hall tree. "There," she said, obviously satisfied; returning, she asked, "Do you take sugar?"

"Yes, ma'am."

"One spoonful or two?"

"Four." He grinned. "I've got a sweet tooth. Besides, we never got enough of anything in the army."

"I know." She sighed. Then realizing how that sounded, she added, "You know what I mean. Army wives are cooped up on small garrisons like this one. There's little enough for women to do even in a city." She paused. "That they're allowed to do, I mean."

His curiosity was genuinely aroused. She was so down-to-earth and natural in her manners that he forgot to be circumspect as men were supposed to be on first acquaintance.

"Like what?" he asked around a mouthful of apple fritter.

She eyed him for a moment, deciding whether she should be frank. She shrugged. "We're never allowed to be natural," she said evasively.

He decided to push her. "For instance? How?"

A perverse elf captured her caution. "Men can go swimming without being bundled up like it was freezing out. They just take off their clothes and jump in the river." Then she blushed. She'd never said anything like that to a man in her life. She was relieved when he laughed. It was a natural, friendly laugh, too, with no hidden implications even in view of her remark.

Dorn was genuinely amused and delighted. "You don't have to go to the city to go swimmin'," he assured her, still grinning. "You could go up the river a ways any day. 'Course the Injuns might be Peeping Toms, but I doubt you'd run into any." He said it all in a matter-of-fact manner.

"That just popped out," she said. "There're lots of interesting people in cities, though. Writers, artists, actors, professional men. All the officers talk about is the war, promotions, and horses."

And while Persephone trundled away the remains of their snack on the muffled wheels of the tea cart, he arose and picked up the book she'd left lying open on a small doily-covered end table by the bow window.

He examined the exterior, which was unaccountably covered in a plain brown paper wrapper. The title page revealed why. It was entitled *The Passion of Lottie Oats* by Letitia DeCoverly. He almost snorted. He could imagine what General Dilly, a true West Pointer, would think if he knew his "little dirl" was reading a book with a title such as this, regardless of what it was really about, which Dorn suspected was anything except real passion. He flipped a few pages and started to read at random: "Roland Armstrong clasped Lottie to his manly breast. She thrilled to the pressure of his arms of steel enveloping and protecting her. He found her lips with his and insistently pressed hard against her. She thought how she'd been told over and over that what she was doing, and thinking, was sinful. A single pervasive notion swept all others from her consciousness—they were fools! She would meet him after dark just as he'd asked her to."

What crap! Dorn thought, laying the book back down.

He was conscious of Persephone Dilly standing close to him. She was a trifle flushed, realizing that he knew what was in the book, but determined not to be defensive. She gave a small, nervous laugh. "Now you know my darkest secret."

He eyed her. "If it is, you'll go to heaven for sure."

"You're not shocked?"

"Hardly."

"You must have led an interesting life."

He recognized that this could be getting him onto dangerous ground in view of who she was. Dilly had hanged guerrillas out of hand during the war and had had deserters shot without the shadow of a legal proceeding. There was no telling what he might do to someone he caught playing patty-cake with his "little dirl," or even looking like he might be thinking about it.

Dorn evaded the leading remark by saying, "Aren't you afraid to leave this lying around where the general might find it?"

"He never looks at a book."

Dorn swung his arm around the room, indicating the numerous shelves burdened with military treatises. "How about all these?" he asked.

She laughed. "All eyewash."

He joined her in the laugh. "Like that, eh?"

"Like that." Then she asked, changing the subject, "What did you think of Roland Armstrong?"

"A clever seducer," he blurted out.

The shade of her eyes had deepened to almost pure black as she watched him, waiting for his answer.

"Is that bad?" she asked boldly. Then plunging ahead, she added, "Does it take one to know one?"

There wasn't a whole lot to say to that. Instead, he did what he knew she was inviting, enveloping her in his arms (of steel) and kissing her. He was surprised to learn that she was an experienced French kisser. Most American women, without instruction, kissed with their mouths as flat and inexpressive as day-old pancakes. The message he was receiving from Persephone Dilly's mouth and body would have resurrected a dead man from his coffin and given him definite ideas about increasing the population. Here was a woman who knew what she wanted and when. She wanted it then.

They were interrupted by the sound of the back door banging open, then shutting.

"Damn!" Persephone snapped. "It's Lottie. She shouldn't have been home before noon."

It was just as well for them that Lottie had come banging in when she did.

The general bounded lightly up onto the front porch and inside before either of them saw or heard his approach. By then Dorn and Persephone were a discreet distance apart, but still breathing heavily, as an acute observer would have detected. The unsuspecting general did not. He was firmly of the opinion that any woman he'd ever made love to would never look at another man. And true enough; the Phoebe, for example, had only looked at a few thousand since him, so he was only partly wrong.

"Ah, Marshal Dorn," Dilly greeted him. "I wondered whose horse was out front." He'd hardly got the words out when a pack of hounds burst through the front door, which he hadn't securely latched. They rushed to Dorn in a friendly manner, begging to be petted and were obliged.

"Capital!" Dilly shouted. "A dog lover. You'll have to come hunting with me soon."

A half dozen of the dogs had rushed upstairs and were soon back in full cry behind a black cat, which they treed on top of a tall breakfront. Persephone was apparently used to this sort of bedlam, taking it all very calmly. The hounds had caught her tomcat once and only playfully mouthed it, sensing that it belonged there and, moreover, that they'd probably get their lumps if they seriously hurt it. To make that point Persephone took after the most active one with an umbrella. They withdrew sheepishly, whining and cringing.

"Get them out of here, George," she ordered her husband.

"Yes, pet," he said, dutifully.

Dorn rightly concluded that life with Dilly might be dull for a passionate lady approaching that difficult age but, on balance, wasn't without its moments of frenzy.

"What brings Bat Dorn here?" the general asked after things had settled down a trifle.

"Just thought I'd drop in and pay my respects since I was out this way. I checked up on Jack Crumm's corrals just in case he had any more wet beeves."

He noted the general's look of satisfaction.

"I heard you got another herd that was run off from Cantoon," the general said with a perfectly straight face.

Dorn decided to play that game too. He said, "I spotted one of the rustlers through my field glass. He had long yellow hair about like yours." He paused for a moment, then laughed lightly. "You ain't into rustlin' as a sideline by any chance?"

Dilly joined in the laugh, looking perfectly bland and innocent. He carried it off so well Dorn started to wonder if he'd been mistaken.

"Well," Dilly allowed, "that narrows down the field a trifle. Not too many men wear their hair this way anymore. Went outa style when old Wild Bill cashed in. Maybe folks figured it wasn't lucky." Then he neatly changed the subject. "Leastwise you know the ringleader is Big-Nosed George."

"I'd've brought him in," Dorn said, "but didn't have the manpower. That offer of some troops still stand?"

He was surprised how quickly the general answered. "You bet. Anytime, day or night."

It wasn't the answer Dorn had expected.

Persephone had left them alone to talk business. She returned as Dorn was strapping his pistols back on, preparing to leave. She took his hand warmly in hers at the door, engaging his eyes with a look that could have operated the post telegraph for about a week, Dorn judged. She handed him a paper sack and gave him a broad wink. "Since you liked the fritters so well, there're two wrapped up inside."

He departed, puzzled on all counts, the general's invitation ringing in his ears—"Don't forget to come course the dogs with me."

Dorn noticed the two sentries watching him from their post on the parade ground and observing both the general and his wife waving at him. On impulse he rode his horse across the parade directly past them. He lifted his hat as he passed. Neither said a word. He grinned at the one bucking for corporal. "Any grass started up yet?"

Once out of sight he opened the bag of fritters. Actually there were two inside—along with a perfumed note. He opened it.

It read: "I'm planning to take your advice and ride alone far up the river sometimes—on Tuesday and Thursday when the general has military training all afternoon. It would be nice to go swimming during this hot spell if I had some protection."

Dorn almost smiled as he remembered the incident. Then he forced himself to concentrate on his escalating confrontation with Big Harry O'Phender.

CHAPTER 15

WHILE Dorn and O'Phender glared threateningly at each other, faraway General Lacey—the Phoebe's father—twiddled his thumbs and longed for a mint julep as he bided his time at the drying-out facility.

The Keeley Institute had a policy of billeting two patients to a room. Usually they put newcomers in a room with someone who'd been there awhile, probably on the assumption that the older patient was well along toward drying out and might be able to keep an eye on the later arrival in case his snakes became too hideous and he tried to flush himself down a toilet, or some such shenanigan. Like the upperclass system at West Point, this one had its occasional failures. Placing Major Pizza in a room with General Lacey, the Phoebe's father, was one of them.

General Lacey had had no idea of the true source of the money on which his daughter supported him. He understood she was happily remarried to a western entrepreneur, although her new husband never came along when she visited him.

Of course the general was a trifle foggy on all details anyhow, and had been since the late, great war. The Lost Cause had stripped his mental gears irreparably, at least in some respects. Even when his wife was still alive and had kept him sequestered in her parlor house, he had embraced the illusion that it was a genteel boardinghouse. Liquor had helped, no doubt.

The general was not without his virtues, however. He was as brave as a tiger. And he was a man of honor from the old school. Above all, that meant he held womanhood sacred, so long as the woman was genteel, white, not his mistress, and not given to dipping snuff, a habit he abominated. He'd once known a quadroon who smoked cigars, but that hadn't bothered him, particularly since she was both beautiful and obliging in his particular case. He himself smoked cigars, the finest Havanas his daughter could afford, sometimes as many as a dozen a day.

When they first brought Pizza into the general's room, Lacey took one look at the major's Yankee uniform and shouted, "Don't bring that blue-bellied son of a bitch in here."

One of the old sergeants who had accompanied Major Pizza that far, a veteran of the Army of the Potomac, grabbed the general by his skinny neck and choked him a little. "Skin that back, you scrawny old rebel bastard," the sergeant demanded. But the old man wouldn't do it.

The major had come to his senses enough on the way down so that he was able to intervene. "Let him go," he ordered.

" 'Druther die first" was the first thing the general said when he got his breath back. The Keeley male nurse had been speechless. He finally collected his wits. "Here, here," he said, "this won't do. The war's over."

Getting the drift of the problem, Major Pizza said, "I never fought the Confederacy. I was in Garibaldi's army then."

General Lacey's ears pricked up at that. As a practitioner of the chivalry of the Old South, he identified with Italy, the ancient seat of classical learning.

"You don't dip snuff, do you?" he abruptly inquired of Major Pizza.

"Heaven forbid," Pizza protested.

"Smoke cigars?"

"I'm afraid so."

"Y'all cain't be all bad, then," the general allowed. "I reckon it'll be all right fer him to move in," he told the attendant.

The two sergeants departed, taking the army's straitjacket with them. The one was still eyeing General Lacey murderously as he went through the door.

"What druv y'all to drink?" Lacey inquired without preamble.

Pizza sighed, rolling his romantic Latin eyes. "What else? A femme fatale."

The general figured that must be some sort of European horse and sympathetically offered some encouraging information. "I ain't bet on a hoss since the wah ended." He obviously intended to imply that the habit was correctable.

Pizza looked a trifle startled, then got the drift. Remembering General Dilly's rare erudition, Pizza asked the general, "Would you be a West Point man by any chance?"

Lacey drew himself up straight. "I am, seh. Class of 'twenty-nine, along with Bobby Lee."

"Ah," Pizza sighed. "A great general, Lee—a great man." He had spotted Lacey's box of cigars and added, "I'd smoke to that but I'm fresh out." The ploy worked.

"Here, seh." Lacey proferred his box. "Have a Havana on me."

Pizza idly noted they were the same brand the Phoebe had once kept on hand for him. A small nostalgic tear formed in the corner of one eye, and he surreptitiously brushed it away.

Thus what was to be an unlikely, but warm, friendship was initiated between a true Damnyankee hater and a bogus Damnyankee.

Pizza was beginning to feel at home, hopeful that he might survive his stay at the Keeley without insupportable pain.

"How's the food here?" he asked.

"Not bad," the general stated. "Not enough okra and grits and red-eye gravy, but tolerable."

Major Pizza had joined the U.S. Army early enough to have served with the occupation forces in the South. He knew what the general was referring to and uttered a small, silent prayer of thanks for the omissions on the menu. Pizza had found the South's lack of appreciation for pasta truly appalling, not that the North was any great improvement over it.

"Do they serve spaghetti here?" the major asked.

"Never heard of it," the general stated.

Pizza thought, "It figures." He consoled himself with the further thought, What the hell, the cigars are good, if I can keep buttering up this antedeluvian fossil.

What Pizza needed most just then was a drink. It was what he was least apt to come by. Like most alcoholics he wasn't about to give up that easily. "Is there any way to get a drink in this place?" he asked.

"Water," Lacey said.

"I've got money."

"They can't be bribed. I've tried it. Damnedest bunch of dedicated cold-water army bastards you ever did see."

Pizza sighed, lying back on his Spartan cot and blowing a cloud of cigar smoke at the ceiling.

"What kind of slow nags was them you said you was bettin' on that druv y'all to drink?" the general asked.

Pizza laughed. "It wasn't horses. I said a femme fatale. That's a woman. It means the same as fatal female does in English."

"Hell, boy. They're all fatal one way or another," the old man rumbled.

"This one particularly. An angel face and a heart of stone."

"Where is she now?"

Pizza hated to think where she probably was—and what she was probably doing with whom.

"Up in Montana near the fort where my regiment is stationed," Pizza said.

"Got a daughter lives up thataway," Lacey told him. "Married to a big-time miner. What's your gal do?"

Pizza hesitated, then said, "She's a dance-hall girl," which was actually gilding the lily.

"A hoor?" the general asked bluntly, just to be sure he'd heard right. But he wasn't shocked. He'd had an affair or two with fancy ladies too in his time.

"A whore," Pizza confessed. "But a woman. What a woman." Tears rolled down his face.

The general was greatly moved. "Take it easy, boy. Time will heal it."

"In this bastille?"

"Even here. But you won't be here forever. I've convinced 'em I was cured a dozen times."

"Don't they get wise?" Pizza snuffled, blowing his nose.

"Of cawse they do, boy. But by now they know I'll be back. My rich daughter pays for it. Nobody gets hurt." His voice sounded forlorn. "Besides I don't have much else to do. The old plantation's grown up in weeds. The house ain't been painted since befaw the wah."

"Can't you go live with your daughter?"

It was Lacey's turn to wipe furtive tears from the corners of his eyes. He realized Breck had small reason to love him, but the suspicion that perhaps she didn't hurt nonetheless. It would have been a consolation for him to know that his daughter did love him with all the warmth that only a bighearted whore can feel. To her he was still a ramrod-straight cavalier in his immaculate gray uniform, fighting with Marse Robert for the Lost Cause. And that's exactly what he was to himself as well, as the kindly Major Pizza soon divined.

Within a week they were fast friends, smoking the general's cigars, lying to each other about the great battles they'd fought, and drinking only cold water. Within two weeks they were like father and son, almost. That's when Pizza got confident enough to bring out his most precious possession. If the general had only brought along a picture of his daughter this time and shown it to Pizza earlier, the tragedy might have been averted—Dorn's tragedy, that is. Pizza was basically a discreet man, but he had not been forewarned.

The general somehow managed to survive the aftershock of seeing the major's photograph of his mature daughter in the altogether.

At first, without his glasses, the general was merely interested. "A demm fine-lookin' filly, boy," he observed. Then, reaching quickly for his specs, he took a closer look. The major misinterpreted his shocked gasp and long, reflective silence. In fact, the general was literally speechless for a long while. He sat on his cot, head in his hands, after hesitantly giving the major back his picture.

Pizza was at a loss. He knew that an old roué like the general couldn't possibly be shocked by a photograph of a nude woman. He wondered if the old man had been tragically reminded of a lost love.

For his part the general had to recognize that it wouldn't be right simply to kill the major, though that had been his first irrational impulse. Even he recognized that none of this was his new friend's fault. He thought of blaming the lady-killer, Bat Dorn, who the major said had stolen his true love away. Such a one wasn't apt to make an honest woman of his daughter. Finally he roused himself and looked at the major. "Would you marry the woman if you could win her back?"

Pizza thought about it briefly, then reasoned that *now* he probably would, whereas he wouldn't have previously when he'd thought he could have her. "I would," he averred stoutly, wondering even yet if he really would.

The general had almost forgotten that his daughter was already married. Then he remembered. Undoubtedly that had been the real problem in the beginning. He had once thought highly of her husband, the dashing *beau sabreur*, Clay Romanza, but he had turned into a weak sot, then had had his stroke, probably from drinking. Clay Romanza had to be got out of the way if Breck was to marry an upstanding officer with a promising career ahead of him—the general's newfound friend, Major Pizza. It slipped the general's mind, if it had ever occurred to him, that the only reason he'd met the major was that he, too, was a weak sot. Whiskey hadn't done a thing to sharpen the general's mind over the years, but a plan was forming in what remained of it.

He grasped Major Pizza's hand and looked him steadily in the eyes. "You've got my blessing, my boy."

The major was a trifle perplexed. "On what?" he asked.

"On marrying the girl, of course."

"Thanks." Pizza had no idea what the old man really meant as the general soon recognized.

He grasped Pizza's shoulder with a surprisingly strong grip. "Look at me," he said starkly. "I'm a dishonored man. Your lost love is my daughter."

Pizza was stunned. Finally he managed to say, "My God!"

"Give me the picture," the general demanded.

Pizza numbly handed over his most prized possession. The general then censored it, in the manner in which it was found later by Pinkerton, using his penknife. He then went to the window and stared out, disconsolately.

"We've got to get out of here. I have a plan," he stated after a while.

Pizza watched him closely and hastily retrieved the cut-out portion of the photograph from the floor, shoving it quickly in his pocket. He thought realistically that it was the part any man would want to remember most anyhow.

"We've got to get down to the Tupelo sanitarium somehow," the general muttered.

Pizza had no idea why, or even what the Tupelo sanitarium was, or where, and he hesitated to ask. "My fate is in your hands," he said humbly, inwardly hedging the pledge with the reservation, "at least till you get me out of here."

"We've got to get rid of her husband," the general muttered.

"Whose husband?"

"The Phoebe's—I mean Breck's—my daughter's. Sally's."

Pizza had told the general about the famed name, Phoebe. He was beginning to be sorry he'd told him anything, faced with the dawning truth that the old man was, perhaps, insane.

"I didn't know she had a husband," Pizza confessed lamely. "Why do we have to get rid of him?"

The general explained at some length, concluding with "So you can marry her and retrieve her lost honah."

"Oh," Pizza responded weakly. He thought, Good luck, old boy! He very badly needed a drink and resolved to get one, a big one, as soon as the general showed him how to get out of this dismal prison.

Whether the general was totally mad or not, he was already displaying the cupidity the mad often possess. He unerringly led the major outside into the concealing darkness through a series of passageways, some of them in the basement. Grimy but free, they gained their liberty at last after climbing up a coal chute. The general kept a talonlike grip on Pizza's arm.

"Now we've gotta make it to the railroad depot. There's no time to lose."

For his part Pizza would have liked to lose a lot of time, or else lose the general, but he recognized it wasn't going to be easy. The wild look in the general's eyes made Pizza fearful of the old man. Moreover, somewhere on their way out the old boy had acquired a long, deadly bowie knife, probably from some cranny in the basement known only to longtime residents such as he. He flourished it under Pizza's nose.

Pizza started sweating, although the night was reasonably cool. All he'd brought with him was the clothing he wore, his money, the photo of Phoebe's midsection, and a box of the general's cigars.

The disappearance of General Lacey and Major Pizza created one of the most hellacious excitements ever to occur at the institute. Luckily they were able to keep the news out of the papers, even though they called in Pinkerton's to retrieve the escapees. As it happened, William Pinkerton himself was in Kansas City on the trail of the James boys. His first notion was to call it kidnapping and hang the rap on the James gang, along with a robbery in San Diego and another in Bangor, Maine, both of which had occurred on the same day. Pinkerton was aces at a grudge. The elusive James brothers had him severely frustrated. He had even resented the grim-faced posse of Minnesota farmers who had shot the ass off the James brothers' cohorts, the Younger Boys, cheating Pinkerton out of some glory in the bargain. That had been a couple years before, but it still rankled.

"I'll find 'em," Pinkerton promised regarding the general and major. He searched their room for clues.

"Everything is exactly the way they left it," a male nurse assured him.

"What's this?" Pinkerton inquired, snatching up a framed photograph of an angel-faced blond lady. Obviously somebody had cut out a big piece of the picture—practically the whole body. "Anybody know who the lady is?"

No one did. If they'd passed it around Warbonnet it would have been a different story.

As Lacey and Pizza made their way toward the Tupelo sanitarium, Clay Romanza lay sprawled on a canopied four-poster bed in his own private quarters at that institution. Most of the sanitarium's other patients could not boast of such luxurious accommodations, but then, none of them owned a substantial interest in the place. After Romanza had gradually recovered—if he'd really had anything to recover from more serious than a combination of malnutrition and natural torpor—he'd risen in the esteem of the proprietor, the widow Lorena Pulsifer-Jones. He had stood fairly high in her esteem, as a matter of fact, before she'd ever seen him, due to his reputation as a dashing young Murat under Jeb Stuart. After they brought him in, pale and as classically formed as a Greek statue, with dark curly hair faintly tinged with gray at the temples, she had often stood or sat beside his bed and talked to him. She was still young, comely, voluptuous—and lonesome.

After a while the general's widow had taken to holding Clay Romanza's inert hand, sometimes clasping it to her body when no one else was around who might misunderstand or, worse, understand perfectly.

That was what she'd been doing when Clay Romanza first regained his full senses. He thought perhaps he had died and gone to heaven when he figured out what was going on. Lorena could have passed for an angel, gently bathed in the fading light of dusk. At candle-lighting time, Clay slyly squinted at his ministering angel through barely slitted eyes. What he saw and felt certainly aroused his interest. But he was ever the sneaky strategist, pretending to be unconscious still, hoping to see what her full intentions might be.

When she had finished her ministrations and quietly departed he'd wondered, Thunderation! How long have I been layin' here unconscious, missin' all that?

He carefully explored his functions to see if he was all there. He was weak but whole. Surreptitiously he had started exercising in the dark after that every night to regain his full strength.

Several thoughts had occurred to him. He had recalled that the war was lost, after which he'd gone on one long, depressed drinking bout. He remembered his hellacious arguments with Breck over that. He wondered where she was—if she was still alive. Then, recalling some of the things she'd called him, he decided he didn't care. He'd managed to get a look at himself in the mirror on the dresser early one morning. He hadn't aged much. He was glad his ministering angel had put him in a private room. He knew why and had plans for her. But he wanted to tip his hand to her in such fashion as to be allowed to remain where he was. As a true and chivalrous gentleman he had no desire to step out into a ruined land, penniless, and undertake supporting a young wife who'd been born and raised in the lap of luxury. He'd rather the roles were reversed—as they were eventually, after Breck got on her feet—or off of them, as the case was.

The hardest part was pretending to be paralyzed when they shoved soup or gruel into his mouth. He had overheard enough from the attending physician and nurses to know what was supposed to be wrong with him. Using diapers was no picnic either. He was anxious to blow his cover—but not so precipitately as to end up out on the street, however. Finally one evening as Lorena Pulsifer-Jones was ministering to him, he helped her out by wiggling a finger. At first she didn't realize what was happening, enraptured as she was over being allowed by providence to ease the burden of a war hero. Startled, she momentarily froze. He opened his eyes and said, "An angel, I'm in heaven." He reached out and drew her to him, kissing her.

"You're awake. It's a miracle," she whispered.

That had been how Clay made his initial investment in the sanitarium. By the time General Lacey and Major Pizza arrived there some thirteen years later he was a full partner. If he ever had missed his wife, whom he'd come to recall as a shrew, no one ever heard him mention it, least of all the widow Lorena Pulsifer-Jones. Together they grew happier each year—and richer. She even managed to get Clay off the bottle.

Consequently, the invalid wreck that General Lacey figured it would be a Christian mercy to dispose of by some charitable means was strong as a horse, standing near the front gate supervising the Negro workers when his liberating angels arrived. General Lacey recognized him at once and hastily drew back out of sight behind a hibiscus hedge, drawing Pizza after him.

"What's the matter?" the major asked.

The general swore. "Unless I jist seen a ghost, that's Clay Romanza out there looking like a champeen stud hoss."

He peered through the bushes. A new strategy was already beginning to form in his mind because his purpose remained fixed—to retrieve Breck's lost honor and, of course, his own as well. The Lacey family honor always stood right up there next to money in his calculations.

CHAPTER 16

WHILE Big Harry O'Phender was still flat on the seat of his pants in the bar at the Bridgewater, Dorn figured it was a good time to collect the five-dollar fighting fee he'd established for breakage in saloons.

"Before this here waltz goes any further," he told O'Phender, "you're gonna have to pony up five bucks."

O'Phender was still a trifle woozy, shaking his head to stop things from wobbling around and his ears from ringing. In fact a few stars were still lazily swimming around in his vision. The remark about five dollars simply didn't register. Fancy Venere and some of his boys moved in to help Big Harry regain his feet. He brushed them away.

"Git the hell outta here," he growled. "I kin git back on me own feet."

His first try wasn't up to his brag. He staggered around and fell again, shaking the entire building. Venere was having an urgent confab with his henchmen, looking deeply worried. "We gotta do somethin' fast," he said in a low voice to Hank Veal, his chief bouncer.

Veal looked surprised. "It looks to me like O'Phender should do something," he observed, quite reasonably.

It netted him a severe look from his boss. "You like eatin' regular?" Venere asked.

Veal got the point. "Okay, so what do we do?"

"Get the boys to crowd Dorn. Shove him in where he ain't got room to slip away from the big ox. If O'Phender ever clinches with him he'll break all Dorn's ribs."

"Good idea," Veal said. He quietly passed the word to the half dozen other house men who were sprinkled through the crowd.

117

By then O'Phender had hoisted himself up. He wondered why Dorn hadn't kicked his head off when he was down. It was what he'd have done if their positions had been reversed. He eyed Dorn warily, a new respect creeping into his brain—also the beginning of a vague uneasiness. He wasn't exactly afraid; he simply didn't like the idea of taking a whipping. The pain didn't matter, but he hadn't taken a shellacking like that since he'd been a kid in school, the year he'd graduated—third grade, to be precise. He was sensitive about his reputation. He heard Dorn say, "I reckon you didn't hear me. You're gonna have to pony up five bucks if yore plannin' on fightin'."

"What the hell for?"

"In case anything gets busted or there's a doctor bill."

The two were separated by about four feet, O'Phender nearest the bar. "Who says so?" he growled.

Dorn pointed a thumb at his chest. "My rule," he said. He was poised for the big man to launch another attack.

"My ass!" Big Harry O'Phender said, coming at him, arms extended to grab him.

Dorn had also learned a few things about wrestling from those he'd fought in the past. In fact, wrestling and boxing had been pretty much blended in most fights in the early days of the sport, and the tradition still hadn't died. He'd been in plenty of fights too where there were no rules at all. He knew that if he got the right leverage he could throw even a gorilla, or twist him out of joint unless he went along with the hold. Like lightning he grabbed O'Phender's left wrist with his own right hand and instead of resisting his momentum used it to his own advantage, jerking forward and down. Then joining his left arm to the right for double strength, he swung O'Phender's left arm in an arc high over the big man's head and back down behind him, leaping forward to do it. The railroader had to go over backward or have his arm twisted out of its socket at the shoulder. He found himself crashing to the floor a second time. As he went, Dorn kicked him in the back of the neck, not so much to hurt him as to keep him from bashing his brains out on the floor. An anguished grunt issued from the giant Irishman. He lay for a moment, stunned, unable to move a muscle. The lamps were wobbling in his vision again.

Dorn rapidly stepped back and almost went down as someone's leg entangled his. He spun to see who was playing dirty pool and caught Fancy Venere trying to slip back into the crowd.

"All right," he yelled, turning back quickly to keep an eye on O'Phender. "Get the hell back and give us room."

There'd been a muffled ripple of sound among the spectators, the majority of whom had bet on O'Phender but nonetheless were mostly game for a fair fight. They moved back carrying Venere's henchmen with them for the time being.

Upstairs watching, the Phoebe was smiling, but breathing hard, a partisan fire glowing in her eyes, rooting for her champion. For the moment she didn't care whether the Bridgewater was forfeited on a bet or not.

O'Phender was playing possum long enough to gather his senses. He decided to wait until he could see just a single light in each lamp. By that time he would have caught his breath. When he finally got up he planned to pretend he was still dazed. He had figured out Dorn's weakness: the marshal was a fair fighter. If he could just stagger near enough and appear almost out on his feet he figured Dorn would simply watch him at first. Maybe he could get him off guard and lurch close enough to grab him. He wasn't counting on outside help, but was a great believer in capitalizing on any he got—as well as luck that came his way. He figured he was a long way from licked.

His plan not only worked just the way he figured, but someone gave Dorn a shove from behind just about the instant O'Phender was set to grab for him. Dorn swerved to avoid him, but Big Harry got a handful of his shirt and jerked him close. He tried to knee the marshal in the crotch but wasn't quick enough for an experienced brawler who expected it. Dorn swiveled, then tried to return the compliment, but O'Phender shoved him back, still pinioning his wrists. Then he whipped him in close to shift his grip to a bear hug and caught an unexpectedly swift boot heel stomped on his foot. He roared in pain but nonetheless spun the marshal around and slipped a hammerlock on him, intending to snap his neck and cripple him.

The crowd roared, sensing Dorn's imminent finish in this hold, which they all had seen used conclusively many times in the past. Most of them were as amazed as O'Phender to see Dorn simply throw his arms over his head and sit down, falling out of the Irishman's grasp like evaporating smoke. On his way down he arched his head back and delivered a blow to his opponent's solar plexis, then farther down, grasped Big Harry's keglike thighs and dealt him a second blow to the lower abdomen. By arching his head, he was able to throw O'Phender off his feet again, giving himself time to roll free. He quickly scrambled to his feet, remembering the sneaky shove that had thrown him into O'Phender's grasp. He spotted Venere in the front of the milling crowd and decided to keep an eye on him.

He gave O'Phender plenty of time to get set again. "C'mon, you big dumb baboon," he taunted. "Try usin' your fists." He made an obscene gesture at O'Phender, hoping he'd take the bait and stalk him. He cast a quick glance behind himself to be sure of Venere's position, then slowly continued to back away from O'Phender, expecting another one of those clumsy roundhouse blows. O'Phender had also seen Venere's sneaky shove and was anticipating a possible repetition to assist him in putting Dorn away for good. He was watching for the key instant to move and telegraphed his punch, just as Dorn expected. Dorn ducked low and grabbed Venere, jerking him into the path of the mighty blow. The saloonkeeper's teeth splattered around on the floor.

Dorn danced away and yelled to the crowd. "He wanted to

git into the fight right bad. I thought I'd help him. Anybody else?"

No one volunteered just then. In fact Venere's crew were dragging their boss out of the line of fire. Dorn hoped he'd broken the scoundrel's neck.

He spotted Sarge Hoak in the crowd and heard his appreciative cry: "Good work, Bat. Now put him away."

Dorn had been enjoying himself, stringing along his opponent who, he realized, was vastly overrated. Goons like O'Phender usually were since few of those they fought brought anything more to the fray, as a rule, than anger and whiskey guts. He felt sorry for O'Phender in a way. But he wasn't going to give him a chance to get lucky just to please the crowd or his own vanity.

No one seemed to know either then or later who threw the beer mug. It caught Dorn behind the ear. He felt his knees wobbling and the room spinning. He broke his fall with his hands and rolled as fast as his dazed senses permitted. Mostly a desperate fighter's reflex made him aware of what O'Phender would do if he could. This roll prevented him from catching a kick directly to his stomach. It caught his upper arm instead, knocking him onto his back. He could see O'Phender's huge bulk launched into a spring to land on his chest with both feet. There was no time to roll farther aside, nor did he have the strength to do so. Only fighting tenacity enabled him to swing his feet upward, deflecting the pounce. Neither of O'Phender's feet hit the mark and instead he straddled Dorn for a second, off balance. Dorn delivered a punch from the floor to where he figured it would do the most good. He heard O'Phender's anguished, "Ooooo!" and saw him stagger away, holding his offended part.

It gave Dorn time to regain his feet. His left arm felt as if it might be broken. He recognized that the odds were now more than even, assuming that O'Phender recovered from his current problem and had any fight left in him. He hadn't been sure what had hit him from behind until he spotted the beer mug on the floor. It suggested to him that he'd better take command of the situation and move the fight outside. It would limit another sneak shot at him by one of Venere's crowd. He could have finished the fight then, he realized, by simply delivering a swift kick to the same place he'd punched O'Phender, but it wasn't his style. The dire emergency was past. Besides he recalled that pick handle outside, leaning against the building. Crippled as he now was, it would come in handy as a last resort. If O'Phender could use the boots, he could use Whang Leather Smith's trusty weapon. Obviously O'Phender was a believer in the go-as-you-please system. The pick handle would have its place if things got desperate.

"Okay," Dorn yelled. "Next round outside. Some of you boys bring a bunch of the lamps."

Upstairs the Phoebe felt a twinge of disappointment. Like the Roman noblewomen who went to the Colosseum to see the gladiators, her blood was up. Then she realized she could probably observe unseen from the upstairs windows just about as well.

As they all moved outside, Dorn hoped no overeager spectator would step around that darkened corner and find his pick handle. There was a breather while the lamp holders spaced themselves out to form a ring with one side up against the building. Cantoon took the stage, flanked by Sarge Hoak. He yelled, "If there's any more dirty stuff like that beer mug, I'm gonna take a hand in this affair and the coroner'll be workin' on some son of a bitch in the mornin'. And the same goes for any more shovin'. Keep the ring clear."

By that time O'Phender seemed to be spry enough. Dorn suspected that Big Harry probably didn't feel any better than he himself did. His left arm was stiffening rapidly. He wondered if he'd be able to use it on that pick handle. He flexed it to try to limber it up. The effort was very painful and not at all helpful. Well, he thought, I've still got my right. I dropped him once with it—I can do it again.

The problem was to suck the other into just the right position to unload. The two opponents now circled each other warily more like two regular ring contestants. Dorn tried to lead with the throbbing left arm, but could hardly hold it up. O'Phender seemed to recognize his predicament and tried to grab that arm a couple of times, rather than box. Each time Dorn swung a haymaker right and missed. He discovered that it was awkward to uncork the Sunday punch unless it followed a left. The problem was both in balance and in getting his feet set. Well, he'd just have to get on his horse and tire O'Phender out. That wasn't hard to do, but it annoyed the crowd.

"Cut the Fancy Dan stuff," someone yelled. A rumble of assent ran through the crowd. Dorn thought of his pick handle, still wondering if he could manage it. He'd have to use both arms; it would be too awkward with just one. He maneuvered O'Phender over to that corner of the building which also served as one corner of their informal ring. His half-formed plan didn't work out in his favor, however. In avoiding one of O'Phender's flurry of blind punches, delivered in a headlong rush, Dorn sidestepped deftly, only to see the big Irishman stumble around the corner into the darkness.

He heard his pleased cry and wasn't surprised to see O'Phender return swishing the pick handle as deftly as a small man would flick a quirt. As a railroader he had practically teethed on picks and sledgehammers and had built up exactly the muscles needed for swinging one naturally.

O'Phender eyed him with a sort of evil, yet amused, anticipation. "You wouldn't happen to know who hid this little shillelagh over there, now wuja?"

Big Harry felt his self-confidence returning. If Dorn

needed a club he must be in a lot worse shape than he had appeared to be. In fact, the railroader had almost been resigned to taking a whipping.

Dorn grinned, trying to project a sense of confidence he by no means felt. He replied to the jibe, "Probably yur friend who threw that beer mug planted the pick handle out there."

O'Phender's face got red. "I din't ask innybody for help."

He swung his weapon then, and Dorn was just able to dodge it. His superior legwork was negated by the reach the pick handle provided the other. He speculated on his chances of stepping inside a swing and decking the Irishman. It was really his only option. As he dodged another swing, he made his move. Perhaps O'Phender had anticipated such a response. He caught Dorn's left leg at the knee with a swift, vicious backswing. Dorn went down on the boardwalk next to the building.

A triumphant grin spread over Big Harry's homely Irish phiz as he stepped up to deliver the coup de grace. Dorn braced himself to fend off the blow with his arms, perhaps grab the weapon if he was wildly lucky.

O'Phender simply had to gloat a trifle. "If yer a good boy I may not split yer skull wide open. Are you a good—"

Dorn saw the pink-flowered pieces of heavy pottery scatter on the boardwalk. He had heard the heavy, dismal kerchunk that preceded them—but he didn't figure out what it was till the fetid smell accompanying the pot's splattering contents penetrated his consciousness. He saw O'Phender disjointedly pour down more or less gently onto the walk beside him. The Irish behemoth was in dreamland from a well-directed bombing by a heavy, very full chamberpot.

Dorn craned his neck to see who had catapulted it down. An open window yawned overhead, but no one was in sight.

The Phoebe had stayed just long enough to be sure her aim was true. In case it hadn't been, she had had two additional rounds in her magazine. They were later found beneath the windowsill. But who had placed them there, or fired the fatal projectile that laid low Big Harry O'Phender, remained forever a mystery in Warbonnet, since Dorn's warm relations with the Phoebe were known to very few. Even the suspicious Fancy Venere, when he regained consciousness and learned of the night's events, had no inkling who the culprit might have been.

Sarge Hoak, never one to miss a chance to gloat over a triumph, visited Venere the next day at Doc Carruther's rude little hospital. He carried a small withered bouquet of prairie flowers as a crowning insult, having picked only those that were on their last gasp. These he'd shoved into the neck of a beer bottle.

Venere could barely talk, but Hoak could make out his "Wadda 'ell d'you wan'?" clearly enough.

"Come to collect on our bet," Sarge said.

Fancy would have grinned except that it hurt. He said, "What bet?" but it came out like "Wah beh?"

"Waddaya mean what bet, you son of a bitch?" Sarge exploded. "You know damn good and well what bet."

At that Fancy forgot himself and actually did grin, then spontaneously grabbed his aching jaw.

"Do I? Who else does?" though it came out about as muddled as his previous remarks. Nonetheless Sarge understood him, drew back his hand as though to hit him. Fancy cringed away. " 'elp! 'elp!" he yelled. This brought Doc to the door. "He tried to kill me!" Fancy got out, pointing at Sarge.

The doctor wouldn't have minded so much, but he'd rather have had it happen somewhere else.

"I'm goin'," Sarge said. On the way out he grumbled, "Somebody really oughta kill the dirty crook." But he knew when he was whipped. There'd been absolutely no witnesses to their bet and nothing on paper. Halfway back to his emporium, still fuming, he suddenly altered his course and headed for Marie O'Neal's. Talking to her always picked up his spirits. He'd been seen visiting there quite a lot—by everyone but Dorn. But he knew Dorn was recuperating in bed from huge lumps on his left arm and knee. Both Mattie and Hattie were fussing over him with Injun remedies, the best of which was genuine sympathy.

CHAPTER 17

DORN, like most frontier town marshals, had spent a lot more time checking to see that businesses hadn't forgotten to lock their doors when they closed at night than he had in heroics. He also investigated all noisy disturbances. He was still hobbling around on a cane, a reminder of the tender ministrations of Big Harry O'Phender, when the most pronounced noisy disturbance of his tenure up till that time broke out down at the end of Main Street. He had been about to stop by Marie O'Neal's for his evening breakfast just before going on shift when the din erupted. His first thought was that someone had stepped on a tomcat's tail—a helluva big tomcat at that—or perhaps the butcher was slaughtering hogs, except that there wasn't a hog within five hundred miles as far as he knew. He glanced in the direction of the racket and could see a torchlit scene—a group of people surrounding a wagon. The noise continued. He recognized that what he saw was a typical medicine show wagon. The noise he now identified as the worst organ music he'd ever heard, and the loudest. He couldn't recall whether the town had an ordinance requiring licenses for medicine shows. In fact, when it came down to wondering about it, he wasn't sure the town had any ordinances at all. He let it slide for the moment and went over to Marie's.

Later that evening, after enjoying a home-cooked meal and several helpings of adulation, he escorted the widow and the two children to the medicine show. They looked like a regular family out for some evening air and entertainment, except that the head of the household was wearing two six-shooters. He had one of the kids on each hand and had dispensed with his cane for the first time. Abe was riding it like a hobby horse.

By the time they arrived at the scene of the atrocity the so-called music had stopped for a while and the "doctor" had launched into his spiel. Dorn had heard him from quite a distance away, expounding on the panacea in the bottle he held up in his hand.

"Ladies and gents of this obviously intelligent group, let me assure you that Dr. Terwiliger's Alligator Rejuvenator is good for warts, blind staggers, walleyed fits, fever and 'ager,' biliousness, loss of appetite and hair. . . ."

He was interrupted by a loud, braying voice, "Hey, Doc, d'ya mean it makes yuh lose 'em or git 'em back?"

This out of a large, half-stewed fellow Dorn recognized as one of Yahoo Dave's teamsters. His question got a large horselaugh from his sidekicks who were passing around a bottle of their own brand of rejuvenator. The more respectable crowd of townsmen chipped in a polite ripple of laughter also.

The doctor stopped, by no means nonplussed. He was used to heckling, obviously not new to his business, though he was a good deal younger than the run of medicine men, most of whom were ancient and bearded, in Dorn's experience. This one was cleanshaven, hawk-faced, tall, and lean, with long blond hair much like General Dilly's. His eyes, visible in the torchlight, were deep blue, now sparkling with good humor as he grinned at his heckler. "Well, podner," he replied, "it works either way—depends on what you want it to do."

The teamster was stopped by that for only a moment. He shot back, "How the hell does it know which I want?"

The doctor was still grinning, unruffled. "That's smart tonic, podner. Smartest on the market. It *knows*."

This drew a general laugh even from the fellow's own crowd. It didn't sit too well with him but he shrugged it off for the time being.

"Dr. Terwiliger's Alligator Rejuvenator, as I was saying before this obviously intelligent fellow helped out with his question"—he paused and got a snicker from the crowd and a scowl from the teamster—"is good for a heap of things, including the flabbiness attendant upon old age." This drew another general snicker from those who got his meaning. "It also removes calluses, cures cholera morbus, and restores the youthful color to hair." He paused again and speared the teamster with a pointing finger. "Was you about to ask how it knows what color?"

The crowd chuckled. The doctor waited, then said, "Same answer. Smart tonic. Smarter'n some people." Another general laugh. The remark was to be the doctor's downfall, more literally than he would have cared for.

"Now," he resumed, "I want to give a demonstration of what this tonic will do for your strength. I'll call out my assistants and pick someone from the crowd to show you what I mean. Gentlemen—the weight, please." Two men trundled a heavy weight from inside the canvas-covered wagon.

Dorn was surprised to see that one of the assistants referred to as a gentleman was the young Injun brave, Sitting Rat. An older Injun with him was the boy's father, though Dorn wasn't yet aware of that. Nonetheless, he (and everyone in Warbonnet) was familiar with the older Indian's name; in fact, through the national newspapers, the whole United States knew the name of the dread Chief Snare Drum, of the northern Fau-ka-Weh tribe, allies of the Sioux and Cheyenne. Dorn had often fought this chief and his fearsome horsemen when he was in the army and had found it no pleasure. The chief's presence here was a sad testimonial to how far the noble redman had been reduced in just a few years. Snare Drum had been promised two dollars and a pint of firewater, or, to be more specific, a pint of Dr. Terwiliger's, which had more alky in it than the best bonded hundred-proof then coming out of Kentucky.

The two Injun assistants had trundled out an obviously very heavy pyramid-shaped iron weight with a big iron ring on top of it. The springs of the wagon rocked impressively as they hustled their burden onto the small stage formed by the wagon's oversized tailgate, which was now resting on a stout set of legs. The front of the wagon, of course, was supported by the usual full-width hinge with a long removable rod inside, which permitted the tailgate to be taken off quickly and easily, if desired. A ring on one end of the rod facilitated doing that, a fact pertinent to what happened a little later.

"Now," Dr. Terwiliger said, "a volunteer from the crowd. Any ninety-eight-pound weakling will do." No one stepped forward, so the doctor volunteered someone. "How about you," he said, pointing out Badger's Navel in the front row.

The Indian was reluctant to volunteer, or at least pretended to be. The doctor finally got him up on the stage, which was now crowded since it had on it the small pedal organ, the doctor, his two assistants, the weight, and the new volunteer. He held up his hands for silence. "What's your name, son?"

"Badger's Navel."

"Have you ever seen me before?" the doctor asked the volunteer.

"Yup," he said.

"Are you sure?" The doctor looked discomfited.

"Sure I'm sure. I see you point your finger at me, ask me to come up here, play damn fool."

The crowd roared. The doctor joined them. To the crowd, when they quieted down, he said, "You get what I'm drivin' at. The kid isn't part of the act." He paused a few seconds. "Now, I need another real burly specimen to heft this weight so you know it's no fake."

Sarge Hoak volunteered. He grabbed the ring and tried to hoist the weight. He turned to the crowd, knowing what the doctor expected of him. "It's no fake," he assured them. "If anyone thinks so, come up and try it."

Dorn expected the loud teamster to do it, but was grateful

to see he'd moved on. He'd figured he might have trouble with him and his friends later. That would have spoiled the fun for Marie and the kids, who were taking it all in, quiet and wide-eyed. He'd boosted Abe onto his shoulder.

"Are those real Injuns?" the boy asked.

"You bet," Dorn assured him.

"Now," Doc Terwiliger said, "before I go on, I want to introduce a celebrity, my assistant, Chief Snare Drum, here with us for one night only."

A subdued mutter passed through the crowd. The chief was about as popular as snakebite among a crowd that had had friends and relatives contribute scalps to ornament his tribe's coup sticks. Someone said, "We oughta string the son of a bitch up." It sounded to Dorn like his boss, Sarge. Dorn suspected Sarge would have appreciated the Indian outbreak that hanging Snare Drum would have caused among the northern tribes, bringing in many more soldiers for Sarge to sell supplies to. Apparently some of the others also saw through Sarge's motive. No one took him up on his suggestion.

"And in addition," Doc went on quickly, "I have the chief's son who has been to the Injun school back East and speaks English as well as most of us." Doc didn't mention that his name was Sitting Rat. Instead he said, "I call him Pronto because he's the quickest helper I've ever had. Besides, when I tell him to do something he always says 'Pronto.' Where did you learn Spanish, Pronto?"

"From the Comanches. They got it from the Greasers."

"From who?"

"The Greasers—the European people from Greece who conquered Mexico. I learned about it in school."

The doctor thought he'd let that pass and get on with the show. If anyone suspicioned that Pronto was a trifle mixed up they didn't show it.

"All right. Here we go. You"—he indicated Badger's Navel—"try to pick up this weight."

The Indian brave strained mightily but couldn't get it off

the tailgate, not surprisingly. It actually weighed at least a hundred and fifty pounds. With the water inside, that is. It also had a drain plug that could be hooked up to a hose that barely stuck up through a hole in the tailgate. Empty, it weighed more like ten pounds.

"Now relax, kid. I want you to take a big swig or two of old Doc Terwiliger's Alligator Rejuvenator, then try to lift that thing again in a little while."

Badger's Navel put down about a third of the bottle which Snare Drum then grabbed from him and drained, being a fast man at managing to get a bonus when one presented itself.

"We'll let that go to work on Pronto for a few minutes while I play a patriotic air or two on the organ," Doc said.

He cut loose with what was barely distinguishable as "Dixie," pausing to announce it as "our national anthem." This got a laugh, as he had expected.

Meanwhile, Sitting Rat—or Pronto—was seated on the stage, his blanket pulled around him, unplugging the weight to let the water drain into the ready hose, which funneled the water away to the ground at the other end of the wagon. To provide enough time for that to happen the doctor swung into "The Battle Hymn of the Republic." He announced, "The Irish national anthem—in case there are any poor losers in the crowd." That also got a big laugh. It was an undemanding generation.

Finished, he got up and nudged the weight with his foot. It was still too heavy, indicating that more drainage time was needed. He said, "I usually tell folks how I came to name my Alligator Rejuvenator. Well, I used to have a fighting dog, a pit bull. He could whip anything that came down the pike. I musta won half a mint on him. One spring I was down in Louisiana and matched him against the local favorite in New Orleans. My dog came out in the pit against a scrubby-lookin', ugly little yellow dog with a short, fat tail. Well, folks, I couldn't believe my eyes. That yellow dog took two snaps and left my pit bull in pieces. He didn't even have time to gasp his last."

Doc had the crowd now hanging on every word. He nudged the weight again and found it almost drained, so went on to finish the story.

"Well, you can imagine I was powerful curious about what kind of dog whipped mine, so I asked the feller that owned him." Doc paused to let exactly the proper amount of suspense build up. "Well, folks, you know what that feller told me, he said, 'Before I cut his tail off and painted him yeller he was an alligator.' Don't that beat all?"

The crowd roared again. Doc waited for them to quiet down. When they did he concluded, "So I named my rejuvenator after that powerful, lightning fighter, the alligator. Also sort of in remembrance of my late lamented pit bull." He then turned to Badger's Navel and asked, "Are you ready, kid?"

By that time the firewater had got its work in. "You bet!" the young brave said, eagerly jumping to the ring to lift the weight.

Just then the suspiciously absent teamsters returned and announced what they'd been up to. The loud one had sneaked around and quietly hitched a strong rope to the ring that would pull out the rod holding up the inner edge of the tailgate. On the other end of the rope was a strong mule, held by a teamster with a quirt in his hand, waiting for the word to use it. The loud teamster also had a cigar lit and had puffed on it to get it red hot. Dorn spotted the glow in the dark to one side of the wagon, partially concealed by the organ, but thought it was merely some late arrival finding a spot to watch from—until the teamster held out the cigar and touched Badger's Navel in a tender spot under the breechcloth.

The young Indian let out a war whoop, jerked the now feather-light weight aloft, and threw it several feet over his head. Simultaneously the waiting mule was whipped into action, collapsing the stage. The organ toppled on top of Doc Terwiliger, raising an egg on his forehead and leaving him out cold on the ground. He was the only one seriously hurt.

Dorn drafted some help to get Terwiliger over to the hospital. Doc Carruthers had been among the spectators and supervised the transfer. "Roll that organ out of the way and we'll use the tailgate as a stretcher," he ordered.

At the hospital they got Terwiliger out of his clothes and into a bed. Dorn said, "I'll check his wallet and see if he's got a home address so we can notify his folks in case of the worst."

Carruthers said, "It won't hurt to check, but he isn't about to croak. He's just knocked cold. He sure put on a great show, didn't he?"

Among the miscellaneous items in the wallet, Dorn found a card with Terwiliger's picture glued to it. The card had a fancy star engraved on it and the name "Pinkerton's National Detective Agency," with the agency's symbol—an eye. Under the picture was printed: Special Agent Turk Bledsoe.

Dorn thought, Well, what do you know about that? We must have some big game around here and not know it. The inventory of possible candidates included Cantoon and Big-Nosed George, both at the head of the list. Maybe I'll need a new deputy pretty soon, Dorn thought as he shoved the papers back in the wallet and the wallet back in the detective's pants.

Just then Indian Agent Jack Crumm, who'd been among the spectators at the medicine show, butted in and caught him putting away Terwiliger's identification.

"Well," Crumm said, indicating the unconscious Terwiliger under the sheets, "did you find out who the prone stranger really is?" Dorn had previously noted Crumm's flair for high-flown phrases like "prone stranger."

He kept a poker face. "He's on the level," he assured Crumm. "No alias." Knowing the Indian agent, Dorn added him to the list of people the detective could be investigating.

CHAPTER 18

EARLY the following morning Dorn went down to Turk Bledsoe's medicine wagon. He found Pronto there looking glum.

"What's the trouble, sport?" Dorn asked, clapping him on the shoulder in a friendly manner.

"Is the *pejuta wičaśa* dead?" the brave asked.

"The what?"

"The medicine man."

"Not by a damn sight," Dorn assured him.

Pronto brightened up right away. Dorn was a trifle surprised. He'd figured the Injun was just hungry. Apparently he'd taken a shine to the Pinkerton detective. This could present a problem. Dorn had come to search through the detective's things to see what he could find out about his mission in Warbonnet. He figured he'd better get rid of Pronto who might, out of loyalty, object. He pulled out his notebook and dashed off a note, handing it to Pronto.

"Take this up to Sarge Hoak, and he'll see you get some chuck."

That got rid of Pronto pronto.

Inside the wagon Dorn found Chief Snare Drum and several empty rejuvenator bottles. The chief was snoring monumentally, lips flapping like the strings of an aeolian harp each time he exhaled. Dorn soon spotted what he was looking for—a suitcase. Inside he found some underwear, socks, and handkerchiefs and the censored photo of the Phoebe, which a few weeks before William Pinkerton had found in General Lacey's and Major Pizza's deserted room at the Keeley Institute.

"What the hell do you know about that?" he said, half aloud.

"What?" a voice asked from immediately outside the gateless rear of the wagon.

Dorn jumped. "Caughtcha!" the prone stranger said.

"Bledsoe, you're supposed to be recuperating up at Doc's," Dorn complained.

"I've already done recuperated. Besides, I saw what Doc was planning to feed me."

"What?"

"Nuts and berries."

"Jeezuz."

"You by any chance know who the good-lookin' frail is in that picture you're holding?"

"Maybe," Dorn allowed.

"Maybe what?"

"Maybe, depending on why you wanna know," Dorn hedged.

"Well, I don't see any reason why I shouldn't tell an upstandin' lawman and pilferer. By the way, have you got a search warrant?"

"Two of 'em. Issued in Hartford, Connecticut." He pointed to his Colt six-shooters.

Bledsoe grinned. "Like that, eh? I hear you're good with 'em."

Dorn changed the subject. "So what do you want with the gal in the chopped-up picture?"

Bledsoe told him the whole story, admitting he was a "Pink," finishing with the implied question, "You sound like you might be able to turn her up so I can have a confab with her."

"Since you ain't plannin' no mayhem or legal processes on her, it happens I can. She works down at the Bilgewater."

"The what?"

"Actually, the Bridgewater—it's our biggest joint. I'll take you down and get you properly introduced if you want."

"I can manage."

Dorn shrugged. "Suit yourself. It's the kind of joint where curious folks find themselves out in the alley on their ass if they're lucky."

"And if they ain't?"

"In the Rosebloom River wearin' a tote sack full o' rocks."

Bledsoe grinned. "I'll take you up on that formal introduction offer." He eyed the empty rejuvenator bottles. "The old cuss had himself a party," he allowed. "I kinda feel sorry for all of 'em. Pronto is a helluva good kid."

"Why don't you take him back and talk Pinkerton's into hiring him?"

"I might just do that."

They headed down toward the Bilgewater together, running into Jack Crumm on the way. "Ah," the Indian agent greeted, "the prone stranger and our esteemed marshal. Good morning."

After he passed, Bledsoe asked Dorn, "What the hell was that all about?"

"Our Injun agent, Jack Crumm. Uses fancy words a lot. He called you the prone stranger last night."

Bledsoe snorted. "Pretty close to the fact," he observed.

"How does your head feel?" Dorn asked.

"About like you'd expect."

Dorn got them upstairs by way of the fire escape. The Phoebe looked surprised to see him bring someone with him, so he briefly explained their business.

"Show her the picture," Dorn suggested.

He noted a fleeting expression of startled surprise cross her face when she looked at it. She was a quick gal with an inference. And apprised as she had just been by Dorn of what had gone on at the Keeley Institute, it wasn't hard for her to figure out what else may have happened. She knew her father. He'd be on his way to Warbonnet sooner or later to avenge the family honor if he'd seen that picture, and it stood to reason he was the one who had angrily censored it. She had to talk to Dorn and warn him what to expect.

Bledsoe asked, "Have you any idea how your picture got where it was found?"

"Yes. Major Pizza and I were good friends."

"Any idea why someone would carve up your picture like that?"

"I can't imagine."

"What were you wearing?"

The Phoebe looked pensive. "I think just a plain house-dress."

She pointedly failed to mention the kind of house. Dorn couldn't suppress a grin, suspecting what she'd worn or, more accurately, not worn.

"Why would General Lacey and Major Pizza skip out together? Do you have any idea?"

"Not really," the Phoebe said evasively.

"Hmm," Bledsoe said. "I guess I've come up here on a wild-goose chase. Well," he said, holding out his hand, "I appreciate your cooperation." He smiled as the Phoebe shook his hand, wondering how much she charged. "Oh," he said, "you wouldn't happen to know General Lacey, would you?"

She decided to jolt him, seeing no harm in it and, in fact, hoping he might trace her father down before he ran amok trying to retrieve her honor—and the family's, of course.

"Yes, I do," she told him, and paused like a good storyteller should.

Bledsoe looked expectant, mouth slightly open.

"He's my father."

Bledsoe's mouth fully opened after that.

"Your father?" he repeated, a trifle stupidly.

"Yes," she said, smiling gloriously. "He's really a dear— only sometimes he's a trifle impulsive."

She managed a word with Dorn alone before they left, her

last caution being, "You'll be in danger every minute from now on. Be careful."

At that moment General Lacey was indeed being impulsive, and repulsive, down at the old Tupelo sanitarium. In fact, he was breathing fire and champing at the bit. He'd had a bad few weeks of it down there. In the first place Major Pizza had disappeared the first chance he'd had to get out of range of the general's bowie knife. He didn't put in an appearance again either. He'd sloped shortly after the general had announced himself to Clay Romanza. The general had decided a frontal attack was best. Dragging Pizza along, he had confronted Clay among the hibiscus.

"Clay, is that really you?" he asked.

Romanza looked him over, then startled recognition captured his face. "General Lacey. What a pleasure."

The general said, "I'll bet. I thought you was off your gourd all these years."

Romanza gave him a sickly smile, "Well, I been gettin' on a trifle better lately."

"I can see that for myself." He came right to the point. "You got any idea where your wife—my daughter—is or what she's doin'?"

If Romanza had answered truthfully he'd have said, No, and I don't give a damn. He knew when he had it made. He also recognized, as Pizza had, that the general looked a trifle loony.

"No, sir, I don't," Romanza confessed.

"Well, she's a hoor and she's up in Montana."

That was the last thing Pizza heard. He was already yards away and retreating rapidly, dodging among shrubs and statuary. He broke out into a sweat and a run simultaneously. As one of the Phoebe's best customers, he didn't plan to make Romanza's acquaintance, just in case. He finally slowed down at Atlanta where he'd bummed his way on a freight train and wired General Dilly collect: "Have been kidnapped by a madman. Stop. Details follow. Stop. Request transportation authority back to Fort Littleworth. Stop."

General Dilly promptly wired him the requested travel authorization, to be obtained from the commanding officer at Fort McPherson. The general had sorely missed his carousing buddy and pimp. He took Pizza's claim about the madman with a grain of salt. If he'd said "woman," the general would have been more receptive to the assertion.

Meanwhile, General Lacey was finding his son-in-law even less receptive than Dilly, only in this case to his pleas about honor and that sort of thing. Romanza had had a good number of years to reflect on honor versus comfort and had come to the rather logical conclusion that honor is a pain in the ass. Of course, like all West Pointers, he'd been nourished on the slogan, Duty, Honor, Country. He also recalled that the signers of the Declaration of Independence had pledged to it "their lives, their fortunes and their sacred honor."

He recalled further that the sacred honor had cost many of them one or the other or both of the former. He'd finally got ahold of a little sacred fortune and had no idea whatsoever of losing it. Nonetheless, noticing that bowie knife of the general's, he had no notion of telling Lacey to piss up a rope, which had been the first thought to pop into his mind.

"Come inside, seh, out of the sun and have some refreshment." He thought, I'll get this old tosspot drunk and take that knife. But he said, "We have some first-rate watermelon."

"Watermelon, hell," Lacey growled. "I need a julep."

"We got that, too," Clay said. He was thinking rapidly. If worse came to worst, he could probably keep the general drunk for the rest of his days. He calculated the probable cost and thriftily decided to have him committed instead.

General Lacey didn't beat around the bush. He said, "Breck is a fallen woman. We're all to blame in a way. Hell, the damn wah is to blame as much as we are."

Romanza nodded. He was relieved that the general sounded rational. His relief was brief.

"Nonetheless, we've got to avenge her lost honor."

"How?" Romanza asked, and soon wished he hadn't.

"Some gunman is livin' in sin with her. You've got to challenge him to a duel."

Romanza brushed that off with "I thought you said she was a hoor. How about the few thousand others involved?"

"Too hard to run 'em all down," the general admitted practically. "Besides, it'd cost too much to print cards to send to 'em all." He tossed down his julep and asked for another.

"Good thinking, General. Let's just forget about the gunman, too. It's over and done now. She's obviously forgotten us. Let her be."

"No, by gawd. It's a matter of honor. You've got to fight."

Romanza wanted simply to get rid of the old man and make it to the flower show in Jacksonville on time. He had some prize hibiscuses and azaleas he planned to enter in competition there.

The general didn't realize yet the extent of his problem. Romanza plied him with juleps until the general went to sleep and fell off his chair. Clay then sent for a couple of attendants to slip the general into one of the sanitarium's natty light canvas sports jackets with arms tied in the rear. Then he quickly looked up Lorena Pulsifer-Jones.

"We got a problem, sweetheart," he told her.

She heard his sad tale and fully agreed.

"Pity things aren't like befaw the wah," she lamented.

"How's that?"

"We could dye him with stove polish and sell him down the river."

Clay guffawed, picturing in his mind General Lacey going under the auctioneer's hammer, protesting mightily while some Simon Legree dragged him away.

Lorena's face registered some new, happy thought. Clay

was familiar with her entrepreneurial leer. The widdy Pulsifer-Jones hadn't survived the lean years on an empty head.

"What's goin' through your pretty, scheming noggin'?" Clay asked.

"Why not sell him up the river instead?" she suggested.

"Waddya mean?" he asked, not getting her drift.

She said, "I understand that a lot of people go to Montana and are never seen again. They even had a governor do it. Why not a general?"

"You mean . . . ?"

"Yes. Do what he wants, up to a point."

Clay first smiled, then frowned. "But not till after the Jacksonville flower show."

And that was why General Lacey was breathing fire and champing at the bit down at the Tupelo sanitarium. To assuage his frustration he fired off a formal challenge to Dorn by way of the Warbonnet *Clarion* and signed it Colonel Clay Beaufort Romanza.

Louis Manner, the *Clarion*'s editor, gleefully published it under a front-page headline reading: "Look out, Bat! Choose Yer Weepons!"

CHAPTER 19

DOC Carruthers, as one of Warbonnet's first and hence most experienced denizens had a habit of saying, "If they aren't here, they're on the way." The reference was to Warbonnet's tendency to act like a magnet for eccentrics, lunatics, exhibitionists, alcoholics, pickpockets, and similarly abnormal people who collectively made the locale energetically useless, but interesting.

Second Lieutenant Harwood Cashing, recently graduated from West Point, fit the mold quite well on the first three counts. He had just stepped down from the Bismarck stage when Chief Snare Drum, recently arisen from his rejuvenator-induced coma, staggered down Main Street in search of manna. Lieutenant Cashing spotted him and, pulling out his long-barreled army six-shooter, blazed away at him with all six rounds. The chief galvanized himself into action right smart, dodging into Hoak's Mercantile unscathed. One lead pill followed him inside, probably lodging in a large cheese, since Yahoo Dave later sank his teeth into a piece of lead in a piece of cheese.

Luckily for the chief, Cashing wasn't much of a shot. The curriculum at West Point ran more to teaching which fork to use for the salad and practicing tourist French. Dorn was just about back to Sarge's place when the shooting erupted, but not quite close enough to shoot the pistol from Cashing's hand. Besides, there was the usual crowd there to meet the stage, and a ricochet could hurt someone even if Dorn did hit the gun. Moreover, he hesitated to shoot the army officer without knowing what was going on. So he trotted over to

Lieutenant Cashing, followed closely by Turk Bledsoe, and asked, "What was that for?"

"That was a redskin!" Cashing announced.

"So what?" Dorn asked. "What did he do to you?"

"Nothing. But I figured shooting him might start an Indian war."

Dorn was puzzled. "Are you tetched?"

"Hell no. But I've got to start a war quick if I'm to make boy general like Dilly did."

Dorn almost laughed. In a way it made sense, but not quite. The subject was too serious. "Do you know who you almost shot? That's Chief Snare Drum. The fact of the matter is he's probably been keeping the peace around here all by himself for the past couple of years."

The lieutenant didn't look impressed. "If that's the case," he countered, "it's time someone else got a little peace, then." He guffawed loudly at his own pun.

Someone in the crowd said, "I like his sentiments. We oughta get him to stand fer Congress."

Someone else said, "It sounds to me like he already does."

Dorn shook his head. "I oughta run you in."

"What for?" Cashing asked.

"Mainly for being a dumshit," Dorn said disgustedly. "Besides, it's against the law to shoot off a gun in town."

Cashing got a trifle red in the face. The charge of being dumb irritated him. At the Point he'd been known as Dandy Cashing and had cut quite a figure.

By this time Chief Snare Drum had come back to look over his assailant. Others were congregating at the scene of the shooting, now that it appeared safe to do so. A grease-stained buffalo hunter edged closer and peered intently at the lieutenant. He said, "You be one o' them martinets, hain't you?"

"I'm a professional officer and a gentleman," Cashing countered.

The chief grunted, "Look more like marshal fella say—

heap dumshit." He stalked regally back to Sarge's store where Mattie and Hattie had been feeding him breakfast every morning.

The buffalo hunter grinned at Cashing. "I'll give you eight to five the old chief thar has yer hair on a stick afore the moon of the popping trees."

"When is that?" Cashing asked.

"Christmas. He'll probably have his squaws tan yer sack as his Christmas present, too, and keep his terbacky in it."

Cashing couldn't believe his ears. "Isn't anyone around here civilized?" he complained, obviously expecting Dorn, as the emissary of the law, to answer.

Dorn pointed east. "St. Paul'd be the closest, I reckon," he offered.

A Dougherty wagon from Fort Littleworth was waiting for the lieutenant, but the driver enjoyed the officer's predicament so thoroughly he didn't announce his presence till the fun was about over. Then he stepped up and saluted. "I've come to drive the lootenant to the fort, sir."

Cashing snappily returned the salute. "Splendid. Splendid. Let's get out of here quickly."

He pointed out his suitcase and trunk to the driver. Once loaded they rapidly drove away toward the fort. Dorn noted the chief, partially concealed a ways back in Sarge's place, evilly glaring after the lieutenant. He scarcely blamed him. "Poor old bugger," he said to no one in particular.

Turk Bledsoe said, "Do you really think the chief'll get his hair by Christmas?"

Dorn grinned. "Who knows? Who cares? It'd serve the young fart right."

Seeing the wagon head toward the fort had brought to Dorn's mind something much more important. In his shirt pocket was a note Persephone Dilly had sent him when she learned of his injury in the fight with Big Harry O'Phender. She'd offered her sympathy and suggested he escort her up along the Rosebloom on one of her rides—as soon as he was up and around. He wanted to be in prime shape when he did. A couple more days would do it, he figured. All of this had occurred before General Lacey's challenge appeared in the *Clarion,* though that certainly would not have changed his plans. He'd already discussed with the Phoebe the possibility that her father might show up breathing fire.

"Don't worry," she'd assured him. "I know how to handle him." She was sure she did—with an almost unlimited supply of firewater at her disposal and several winsome girls who worked at the Bridgewater under her supervision. She knew Papa's weaknesses. She was grateful that Dorn hadn't been the least bit curious about her proposed tactics. The fact was Dorn had developed a great deal of confidence in her competence, based on ample observation. For her part, she didn't wish to have to lie to him, as delicacy would have prompted her to do in this case. Family pride forbade her publicly discussing the peculiar anatomical location of her father's brains. As to the matter of cooling the general down if he showed up, the Phoebe decided that, as a last resort, she would threaten to cut off his allowance. She knew that she was his sole support.

The following morning Lt. Dandy Cashing paid his duty call on General Dilly, as all newly arrived army officers were expected to do. As usual, Dilly was out riding to the hounds. Cashing rang the bell, just as Dorn had, and Persephone again peeked around the lace curtains to see who was calling. She rather liked what she saw just as she had in Dorn's case. It happened that her maid was out again. She answered the door personally.

Dandy Cashing had expected a servant to answer the door. He wasn't prepared for one so lovely, well-dressed, and refined.

"Come in, Lieutenant," Persephone invited in a cultivated voice.

He did, appearing nervous. He was a trifle tongue-tied, ogling the sumptuously furnished foyer and adjoining parlor. "Uh," he said.

Persephone decided not to be helpful. "Uh, what?" she asked.

He blushed. She thought he looked boyish and quite appealing when he did. She'd had secret longings lately to be high priestess at a rite-of-passage ceremony, and she gloated inwardly. She hoped the general and his hounds would stay away long enough, and that Lottie wouldn't come back early again.

Dandy grinned. He'd been told that his smile made him irresistible to the ladies. It had at least helped to get several of them into the bushes in the vicinity of West Point after dark. Deliberately sounding shy, he said, "Uh, is the general in? I'm Lieutenant Harwood Cashing." He placed his card properly on the silver salver that stood on a piecrust table inside the door for that specific purpose.

"The general is out. I'm Mrs. Dilly." She held out her hand graciously, and he shook it equally graciously, holding on a trifle longer than custom prescribed. He felt a strange sort of magnetic impulse leap from her hand into his body, which localized at about where the buffalo hunter had suggested he had the raw material for a tobacco pouch.

Persephone eyed him intently, trying to look severe as she pulled her hand away. "You're rather a fresh case," she told him.

"I'm sorry," he apologized humbly. "I don't know much. I was an orphan."

What he did know was that both of those ploys were almost as appealing as his boyish grin, or perhaps more so. Women immediately melted, deciding to mother him. He could read the change along that line in Persephone's eyes. Dandy Cashing was no fool.

"Well," Persephone said, smiling, "we can start your social education now. It's part of the duty of a commanding officer's wife, as a matter of fact. Come in and have a seat. I'll fix some coffee, or would you prefer tea?"

In truth he would have preferred a big slug of Kentucky sour mash, but he said, "Tea, please."

She caught him watching her fascinating wiggle as she went to get his tea, just as she had caught Dorn. Persephone, old girl, she told herself, this day is beginning to show some promise. She'd been afraid it would be just another day spent alone with a forbidden novel.

After they had partaken of tea and fritters, she sighed. "Well, I suppose you'll want to rush back to your new company and get your career started. No telling when the general will be back. Probably after dark. It gets boring for a wife out in this godforsaken country."

"Yes, ma'am," he agreed. "I'll bet it does. If there's ever anything I can do to help brighten up your day, I'm at your service."

He rose to make his departure, not really wanting to leave.

"Oh," she said, as though just remembering it. "You can help me bring a trunk down from upstairs before you go. I have some things to ship to my sister back East. You look so strong." She playfully felt his arm muscle, and he had another terrible twinge in the tobacco pouch.

She led the way upstairs, then to a third-floor spare guest room set in a large attic dormer. Dandy noted that the room was fully furnished, including a large bed.

Persephone giggled. "I guess I'm not a very proper social tutor, leading a strange man into a bedroom, am I?"

For all of his prior experience in the bushes, Cashing wasn't sure how to take that remark until he observed her flushed face and the warm invitation in her eyes.

She stepped close to him and placed her hands on his chest. "You are strong," she said.

He took her into his arms, gave her a preliminary demonstration, and was as amazed as Dorn had been at her proficiency in kissing. She slipped away for a moment and locked the door.

The engagement had just reached its tenderest moment when General Dilly and his hunting party thundered up in front of the house on their horses.

Persephone leaped up and scrambled into her clothes as fast as she could. She knew the general would let the dogs inside and that they'd soon track her down. Then the general would rush in and kiss her as though he were returning from the wars.

"Quick," she directed Dandy, "get your things and hide way back in the closet. The hounds will be up here in a minute, and so will the general." She got dressed just in time and put on a show of trundling the big trunk onto the landing at the head of the stairs. This explained her somewhat disheveled appearance, or at least she hoped it did. She saw the general at the foot of the stairs, which by then were crowded with hounds.

"What in the world is my turtledove doing?" he asked.

"Moving this trunk that I've been going to send back to my sister."

"Leave it there, for goodness' sake. I'll have some enlisted swine come over to move it later and take it in to Wells Fargo."

Relieved, she made her way down the stairs, driving the hounds before her. She hadn't noticed that two of them had nosed their way into the spare bedroom. As she departed the stairwell, carefully closing the door, her mind was already racing on the problem of how to get Dandy out of the house. She needn't have worried—at least not on that specific point. The two dogs left in the spare bedroom were soon barking "treed."

"What the devil is that about, I wonder?" the general asked.

He didn't notice Persephone's agitated look. She got an instant mental picture of the similar scene in *Don Juan* and hastily headed for the stairs. "I guess I left two of them up there. They've probably treed the cat again."

"I'll go see," Dilly said.

"No, dear," she insisted. "You're tired from your ride. I'll go see."

She swiftly left before he could object. Getting the two dogs away from their quarry to come downstairs with her wasn't easy. Before she left she managed to tell Dandy through the closet door, "Get into the trunk. I'll get you out of the house as soon as I can."

That evening the Warbonnet Wells Fargo agent heard the pounding and muffled cries from inside the recently deposited trunk. When he liberated Lieutenant Dandy Cashing, he didn't have a stitch of clothing on, although he had managed to get his uniform inside the trunk with him. He'd been almost asphyxiated by the smell of cedar and the lack of fresh air, but fortunately for him the trunk hadn't been airtight.

The agent looked startled. "What the hell happened to you?" he asked.

"I was abducted."

The agent wondered what sort of perversion that was. He'd heard of a lot of them at some of the fancy houses downtown. The young man didn't seem any the worse for it in any case. "Can I get you anything?"

"Whiskey."

The agent produced the office bottle, watched Dandy drain a big slug, then start to get into his uniform.

"Hey," the agent said, "you be that martinet that tried to shoot the chief yesterday, hain't you?"

"That's me," Dandy admitted. He fished out a gold fiver and handed it to the agent. "This is a little something so you'll keep this embarrassing incident to yourself," he said. "They'd laugh me outa the army if anyone heard. Some of the other lieutenants did this to me as a joke."

"Oh," the agent said. "I git it." He wasn't sure what being abducted involved, but he was a trifle disappointed. "Mum's the word," he promised, planning to tell everyone he met as soon as the lieutenant was gone. He'd been a private in the Army of the Cumberland for three years during the Civil War and hated officers with ample reason.

Outside, the lieutenant stole the first horse he found

tethered at a hitch rack. He didn't see young Pronto pretending to be asleep, propped against the nearby saloon wall. But Pronto saw him. Turk Bledsoe, not willing to give up on the mystery of Pizza's disappearance, had sent his faithful Injun companion down to snoop, instructing him to keep his eyes and ears open.

"Ah," Pronto said. He pulled out a turnip watch he'd once pilfered from a dead cavalryman and noted the time, then wrote something in a small notebook, just able to make out what he was doing by the spillover light from the saloon's interior. "Plenty good," he said. "Prone Stranger say watch saloon. Watch plenty good, but saloon heap still. This look better." Pronto pretended once again to be asleep, floppy hat pulled over his eyes.

Lt. Dandy Cashing still had a few days' leave coming if he wanted to take them before joining his company. What decided him to take at least one more day was seeing Persephone Dilly ride her horse out of the fort alone. He then had his own mount saddled and followed in the direction he'd seen her take. By then she was out of sight. He didn't have the foggiest notion how to follow a horse's tracks. Neither did he see Dorn cut the trail of Persephone's mount a half mile ahead of him, although both of them were on an open prairie at the time. By pure happenstance the lieutenant stumbled across the Rosebloom River in about another hour. He hit it very near the grove of huge cottonwoods where Dorn had overtaken Persephone.

Once inside the tree border, Dandy Cashing heard the merry sound of laughter accompanied by happy shouts and splashing water. He did have enough caution to dismount, tie his horse, and try to slip up on the spot the sounds were coming from. He was cautious only because of the unexpected nature of the sounds out here in what he considered to be a dangerous howling wilderness. Perhaps Indians were cavorting. He drew his six-shooter and tiptoed through the dense, low-growing willow bushes and tall grass.

From one particular bush, he heard an urgent feminine

voice gasping, "Oh, Dorn! Oh, Dorn! Oh, Dorn!" He was familiar with the biblical story of the voice in the burning bush, but he didn't think that was exactly the case this time, though in one sense a burning bush was involved all right. He saw a pair of small feet wiggling in the air. Then he realized he had heard that particular female voice before. Carefully he parted the bushes and found himself looking directly into the eyes of Persephone Dilly. It was fairly clear what she was doing. Her final, "Oh, Dorn," was said in a different voice, as a warning.

A sudden rage captured Dandy Cashing. He was the jealous type.

"Come out of there and defend yourself, Dorn!" he cried.

Dorn came out of there—unavoidably—rising and viewing the lieutenant disgustedly. The officer put up his dukes in the classic manner.

"Shit!" Dorn muttered disgustedly.

He decked Dandy with one sneaky left, knocking him out cold.

"Let's get out of here," he suggested to Persephone. He started to lead the way back to their clothes.

"You go ahead," Persephone said. "I'll be right with you."

He was a trifle puzzled but did as she said. He was sure the lieutenant would be out cold for a while. He heard a small industrious thrashing around back in the bushes, which were located on a cut bank a good ways above the water. Shortly he heard a subdued splash. That, too, was a trifle puzzling. If he'd had greater experience in the matter he'd have recognized the dismal splash of an unconscious second lieutenant being dumped in a river by a small, determined woman. The water very shortly revived Cashing. He came up sputtering. By the time he was able to find a bank low enough to climb out on, he was a couple of miles downstream, almost exhausted. There Pronto and Bledsoe, out coursing the country, spotted his struggling form and threw him a lariat.

"What the hell happened to you?" Bledsoe asked him.

"You wouldn't believe it if I told you," Dandy said.

Pronto pointed an accusing finger at him. "You be that martinet that took a shot at my pa," he accused. He turned to Bledsoe. "Let's dump his ass back in the river."

It was a hell of a hard country on second lieutenants.

CHAPTER 20

GENERAL Dilly got a short note through the U.S. mail. It read:

Dear General Dilly,
You might be interested to know that your wife frequently goes riding alone up along the Rosebloom River.
A Friend

The general read it over a second time. He'd been around long enough to know that this wasn't simply a note from someone concerned that possible harm might befall his wife. The implications, judged by reading between the lines, were that a sore loser was mad because Persephone was now playing patty-cake with someone else. He couldn't really believe that either implication had foundation in fact. This had to be some spiteful person who was trying to get his goat. Or was it? Persephone was too contented and wholly without guile to be capable of what was being hinted. Or was she?

The general was pondering these questions when Turk Bledsoe was announced by an orderly, who asked whether the general wished to see the man. The orderly had already handed the general Bledsoe's card.

"Send him in," the general said. The name Pinkerton commanded attention almost worldwide. In fact, the general had known Allan Pinkerton when he was General McClellan's secret service chief.

I wonder what the Pink wants? Dilly speculated inwardly.

He considered his own record and dismissed the notion that he could be a subject of investigation. Of course, he had been speculating in stolen cattle, on the one hand, and taking a payoff from Major Bulstrode, the post sutler, on the other, but he was sure that those in the know—the major and Jack Crumm, the Indian agent—hadn't spilled the beans.

The general was still turning over in the back of his mind the note concerning his wife. He shoved it in a desk drawer and pretended to be studying Bledsoe's card when the detective entered. Dilly remained behind his desk, rising to shake hands briefly. He looked questioningly at the detective but remained silent except to ask him to be seated.

Bledsoe surprised him by not beating around the bush even for a second. "I'm here for two reasons. First we've been employed by the Keeley Institute to find a member of your command that you sent down to dry out. He's disappeared."

That was blunt enough for anyone.

"Ah, yes," the general said. "Major Pizza."

"The major somehow broke out, accompanied by an old Confederate fire-eater, General Lacey," Bledsoe said.

"I know," Dilly told him. "The institute wrote me."

"Do you have any idea where either or both of them may have gone?"

"Yes, as a matter of fact, I do."

Bledsoe's expression registered mild surprise. His opinion had always been that the army, individually and collectively, couldn't find its ass with both hands. It was an opinion pretty universally shared by anyone who'd ever been in the army and possessed the wit to escape.

The general continued, "As a matter of fact, I not only have an idea, but I know precisely where they went."

He paused so long—deliberately—that Bledsoe asked, "Do you mind telling me where?"

The general's eyes twinkled. "Not at all," he said. "They went to a place called the Tupelo sanitarium."

"What for?"

"I don't know, but I have an idea who can tell you. Major Pizza is due in any day now. He wired me for funds to get back."

"Are you planning to send him back to finish the cure?" Bledsoe asked.

"I doubt it. I think he just needed a little time to forget a woman."

"And you think he's had time?"

The general nodded. "He was already calling her old what's-her-name before I sent him down there."

Bledsoe laughed. "Well, I guess that closes my case on him. I'll wire Chicago and let them know. That brings up my second little matter of business."

The general raised his eyebrows expectantly as though to say, And what's that?

"Cattle stealing."

That got a little fundamental puckering out of Dilly, which he tried to conceal with an impassive face. He was wondering what the chances were that the detective could be bribed—and who had squealed. Probably Bulstrode, certainly not Crumm, since he himself could go to jail for what they were doing. Bulstrode would not. The son of a bitch! he thought.

He was rescued from that unhappy train of thought by Bledsoe's next remarks. "I'm after a fellow named Big-Nosed George Chutney."

"For rustling?"

"Also bank robbery. Mr. Pinkerton thinks he may secretly be one of the James gang." Bledsoe reflected wearily that Mr. Pinkerton thought almost everyone might secretly be one of the James gang.

"You don't say. I've heard of Chutney."

"I'm not surprised."

"Yes," the general went on. "Marshal Dorn caught him running off a herd but didn't have enough manpower to capture him."

"That's one thing I came to talk about. I may need some help when it comes to bringing in him and his gang."

Dilly felt vastly relieved. "Count on the army if you need us," he said. He realized that using the army as a posse would be illegal, but legality meant as little to Dilly as it did to most frontier officers. They'd got away with so much they'd come to believe they were a law unto themselves—and they were. The question was whether they could continue to get away with it indefinitely. Few of them worried about it.

Bledsoe rose, mission completed. "Well, General," he said, "I'd be pleased if you'd let me know when Major Pizza returns. I'd like a chat with him."

"I'll do that," Dilly said. He also made a note to be sure he was present at that chat. Something about this whole thing disturbed him. Bledsoe had explained his presence well enough, but Pinkerton's men, or any detectives, were not to be trusted. For all he knew, Major Pizza may have resented his enforced trip in a straitjacket and made some accusations that would prompt division headquarters in Chicago to dispatch a Pink to investigate Dilly himself. The army had used the detective agency before.

General Dilly meant to keep this matter foremost in his thoughts. But after Bledsoe left, the general's mind returned to the troubling note about his turtledove.

Dandy Cashing wanted to savor watching the general catch Dorn in the act, particularly after that punch in the mouth and his impromptu swim in the Rosebloom. He, of course, thought Dorn had flung him in the drink. Ever since he'd sent his note to the general, he'd been trying to catch Persephone leaving the fort on her horse. He assumed the general would also be on the lookout. When a couple of days passed without perceptible sign that the general was acting as though he'd received the note, Dandy grew restive. He wondered if the mail service had lost it. The third day after the note's arrival, curiosity overcame the lieutenant. He'd seen the general and his usual hunting partners depart with the hounds—in the opposite direction from which Persephone always rode, at that. Later he watched her leave the fort on her horse and shortly thereafter followed, first heading toward town, then making a wide circuit, out of sight of the fort, to intercept her.

She rode to the usual spot and disappeared into the trees along the river. Dandy hid, waiting for Dorn's arrival. He had no idea what he planned to do, if anything, besides watch, but he couldn't leave until he was sure what was going on. He also wanted to see if the general showed up by a roundabout route. After a couple of hours had passed he decided to follow Persephone's trail to see if perhaps she'd returned to the fort unobserved. He found her happily paddling in the river. At the sight of her and the recollection of her warm, resilient body in his arms only a few days before, caution deserted him. He completely forgot his strategy.

He stepped out in plain sight on the riverbank.

"Mind if I join you?" he asked.

She jumped at the sound of his voice, automatically settling herself up to her neck in the water. Her eyes narrowed, revealing rapid appraisal of the situation. She knew that Dorn would not be here today. She'd come merely to be alone. However, here was an opportunity. The sensual memories evoked by this site had aroused her blood.

She smiled. "Why not?" she invited.

He was quickly out of his uniform, tossing it on the grass. The swim was short-lived as is usual under such circumstances. Dainty feet were again waving about the burning bush in a short while. Persephone was breathlessly saying, this time, "Oh, Dandy! Oh, Dandy! Oh, Dandy!" when General Dilly parted the leafy foliage above them. She saw him and thought, Oh damn! But she said, "Oh dear!"

Dandy thought she meant him until he felt a saber jabbing his butt. He turned his head, his jaw dropped, and he gasped, "Good Christ! The boy general."

With Persephone as a witness, the general couldn't simply shoot him, but Harwood Cashing was able to boast of one of the shortest military careers on record. His resignation was on the general's desk and a bandage on his haunch, all within two hours. By sundown he was in Warbonnet, out of work. He blamed Dorn for the whole thing and planned to get even. He had a hearty respect for the marshal, however. He knew it wouldn't be easy, but he also knew that Dorn didn't have eyes in the back of his head. Cashing hadn't decided whether to back-shoot the marshal or knock his brains out with a club. In any case he'd always been top-notch at carrying a grudge.

It was the day after Lt. Dandy Cashing resigned before Turk Bledsoe looked up Dorn for a talk. He found Dorn in the rear of Hoak's Mercantile, talking to Hizzoner the mayor. Also hoisting a cold beer.

"Have one," Sarge offered.

"I've sworn off," Bledsoe said.

Sarge, who'd known him for a few days by now, wordlessly uncorked one and handed it to him anyhow. They comfortably rocked back in the chairs Sarge had recently installed for just such occasions. Dorn lit a cigar. "Take me now, Lord," he said, blowing a cloud of smoke at the ceiling. "I wanna go happy." He glanced sideways at Bledsoe, "Well, Prone Stranger, what's on your suspicious, pussyfootin' mind?"

"Nothin'," Bledsoe said. "Naught."

"I'll bet."

"Well, there was one little trifle," he admitted.

"Uh-huh. I thought so. Shoot."

"I got another little job they sent me up here on besides Pizza's case. General Dilly tells me you're practically sure that you caught Big-Nosed George Chutney rustlin'. I want to know who from?"

Dorn decided he hadn't better answer that whole question. Since he'd hired Cantoon as deputy, the marshaling job had been a lot easier. He told Bledsoe, "No doubt about it bein'

Big-Nosed George. I could make him out plain enough. With a little more help I could have run him in."

"Who'd you have along?"

"Mattie, the lady Injun who's been cookin' our vittles, remember?"

"Oh. Yeah."

Dorn had acquired quite a family in the past few weeks. It now consisted of Sarge, Cantoon, Bledsoe, Chief Snare Drum, Pronto, Badger's Navel, Mattie, and Hattie. They were all eating meals upstairs together, except when Dorn took evening breakfast at Marie O'Neal's and morning supper with the Phoebe.

"Well. So we know Big-Nosed George is up here. Now all we gotta do is catch him."

"Easier said than done, maybe. He's pretty cute."

Sarge rose and tossed his empty bottle in a trash barrel. "Gotta git back to work. You two sleuths help yerself to another beer if you want one." He ponderously waddled out.

"We'll catch Chutney sooner or later," Bledsoe said. "Pronto thinks he saw him down at the Bilgewater one night."

"How'd Pronto know what he looks like?"

Bledsoe said, "I showed the Injun a photo just like the one we sent you. Remember? That's how we caught on to where he might be. Pinkerton thinks he's a member of the James gang. Also probably a confederate of the Russian anarchists."

"Do tell? What makes him think that?"

"He thinks almost everyone is one or the other, or both."

Dorn laughed. "Sounds to me like Pinkerton's buckin' for corporal."

"Uh-uh," Bledsoe said. "Pinkerton wouldn't settle for less than God. At any rate he's managed to have a big reward put on Chutney."

"How big?"

"Five thousand bucks, dead or alive."

Dorn whistled. "Pinkerton must want him bad." He wondered how an outfit like the Pinks could talk several governors into offering rewards totaling that much for the dead body of someone who hadn't even been so much as indicted, much less convicted—and who certainly had never killed anyone or, so far as Dorn knew, even hurt anyone. The worst he'd done in Montana was hurt the feelings of Cantoon and General Dilly. Even Sarge thought his tactics were amusing. Dorn thought, They won't get me to bust a cap on him unless I have to do it in self-defense. Besides, with Chutney out of the way the territory would lose out on a good belly laugh whenever he boosted another one of Cantoon's stolen herds.

Dorn's mind shifted back to Pronto down watching at the Bilgewater. He himself had noticed the Indian slumped against the wall, hat pulled down, looking like a shiftless beggar, maybe half drunk. Now it was clear to him why Pronto kept hanging around there, or at least he thought it was.

"I reckon you got the Injun kid workin' for Pinkerton," Dorn allowed.

"Cor-rect. And he's a good man. You'd be surprised how much he finds out. F'r instance, did you know that Fancy Venere don't own the Bilgewater?"

"No? Then who does?" Dorn asked.

"The Phoebe."

"The Phoebe?" That was a shocker.

"Yeah, the Phoebe. Pronto heard her givin' Fancy Venere hell the other night."

"For what?"

"He was aimin' to have you bushwacked fer holdin' his mouth about where Big Harry O'Phender was gonna swing a roundhouse punch."

So the Phoebe owns the joint, Dorn thought. That answered a few questions. For example the big question of why she hadn't worried about whether Venere found out about her affair with Dorn. And why Venere lived in a dumpy cottage at the edge of town while she lived in a sumptuous apartment above the saloon. It could also answer the question of who the lousy shot was that missed him with a double-barrel shotgun a few nights past. The buckshot had gone wide of his head and into the adjoining livery barn, obviously barking a horse, which had then kicked out the wall above where Dorn had hit the dirt.

He said to Bledsoe, "So old Fancy is aimin' to get me?"

"Was. The Phoebe read him the riot act and reminded him where his bread and butter was comin' from. He ate humble pie."

Dorn shrugged. "It don't signify. I'm gonna go down and run him out of town. Wanna come along?"

"Wouldn't miss it."

On their way down to the Bilgewater Bledsoe said, "The general also mentioned that Major Pizza is on his way home. Due any day. I aim to ask him a few questions. Thought you might like to sit in on that."

"You bet."

At the Bilgewater Dorn didn't waste any time. He found Fancy standing at the bar, grabbed him, spun him around, kicked his ass hard, and said, "Be out of town by sundown."

He turned his back and casually strolled out, lighting a cigar with what Bledsoe noted was a rock-steady hand.

"So much for that," Dorn said.

"Don't count on it," Bledsoe cautioned. "He's a sneaky-lookin' devil. I wouldn't put it past him to slip back in and have a shot at you himself."

"He ain't got the guts," Dorn allowed scornfully. "He'll hire it done."

Dandy Cashing hadn't seen the confrontation between Fancy and Dorn, but he came into the Bilgewater shortly afterward. He asked the bartender where the boss was and had him pointed out at the end of the bar, standing alone. Fancy was pondering his next move and knew he was being given a wide berth by even his henchmen, probably in case Dorn changed his mind and returned.

Dandy had been quite a gambler at West Point and hoped to be hired on as a dealer.

"Excuse me, Mr. Venere," he said, "but I'd like to hit you up for a job."

Venere eyed him sourly, especially his ill-fitting civilian suit. Then he recognized him. "You be that martinet, hain't you?" he asked.

"Not anymore. I resigned. No money in it."

Fancy said, "We don't need any more dealers. Sorry."

"I really need a job. I'll do anything," Dandy pressed him.

Venere's face lit up. "Anything?"

"Damn right—if the price is right."

"C'mon back to a table and let's talk," Fancy invited. He motioned the bartender to bring over a bottle and glasses. After the bartender was out of hearing, Fancy said, "You had a run-in with our marshal the other day. How'd you like to even the score?"

Dandy looked instantly happier. "You don't know the half of what I owe him." He gloated at the notion of being paid to get even.

Their heads were together for a while and a substantial down payment changed hands.

Later that day Bledsoe received word from General Dilly that Major Pizza had returned and was willing to talk to him. The detective again sought out Bat Dorn, and the two headed for Fort Littleworth. Dorn knew he'd shot Pizza out of the saddle with the Phoebe and expected to encounter a resentful attitude, but could detect no evidence of one. He shook hands cordially with Dorn.

General Dilly said, "The major has a remarkable story to tell." He turned to Pizza. "Why not just start at the beginning and tell the whole thing just the way you told me?"

That's what Pizza did, not sparing himself and omitting

nothing, not even his retrieval of the part of the Phoebe's picture that General Lacey had cut out.

"I'd like to see that someday," Bledsoe said.

The major withdrew it from his inner blouse pocket. Bledsoe had brought the other part along intending to ask the major about it. This saved him the trouble. He assembled the photo and let out a low whistle. He said, "I can see how the general might have popped his cork seeing his daughter in"—he fumbled for a word—"her housedress, you might say."

Dorn grinned, since he was in on the detective's clever little joke. Pizza sighed, "What a pattern they cut it on, too." It was a strange fact that all of them except Bledsoe had seen the original in the flesh. If the detective had had his way he'd have made it unanimous at the earliest opportunity. He now knew for sure how it was with her and Dorn, but planned to inquire if she still carried a light load, perhaps, to help out the other girls.

"Well, Bat," the general said, "Pizza here seems to have got you in dutch with old General Lacey."

Pizza looked genuinely contrite. "I had no idea the old bastard was the Phoebe's father when I mentioned your name to him. In fact you can bet your hat, ass, and mess kit I'd never have shown him the picture if I'd known who he was."

"You say Clay Romanza looked fit to as a fiddle," Dorn asked.

"Just like old Lacey said—like a prize stud."

General Dilly laughed. "He was always that." They'd been classmates at the Point before the late, great war.

Dorn, who had also known him well, knew that to be true. Clay, he recalled, had been in one mansion or another, squiring the belles, every night there hadn't been a battle or skirmish to keep him from it. Most of the time he'd had Dorn with him. He recalled what a jealous bastard Clay was, as well—and a crack shot. There was little doubt in his mind that Clay Romanza and General Lacey would show up one day soon at Warbonnet, nor did he doubt what their mission would be. Retrieving the family honor. He wondered what Clay Romanza's reaction would be when he found out who Bat Dorn really was. He realized that he'd better get together with the Phoebe so they could plot some strategy. He planned to live a good many more years yet if he could.

On their way back to Warbonnet, Bledsoe, who'd been checking into Dorn's record as marshal, said, "For a likable feller you sure manage to get yer foot in it, don't you?"

"Howzat?" Dorn asked idly, though he'd been thinking pretty much the same thing.

"Want me to count yer newfound friends on my fingers, if I got enough fingers?"

Dorn said, "Go ahead."

"Well, there's Pronto and his buddy, who may decide to get back their tepee, hosses, and gals, for starters."

"You think Pronto's still holdin' that against me?"

"Can never tell. Injuns is funny. Maybe not. He's gettin' plumb civilized though—so's the other one. But not countin' them, there's Yahoo Dave, Fancy Venere, Big Harry O'Phender, Clay Romanza, and the Phoebe's father; maybe even Big-Nosed George since you rustled back his rustled cows. How about Pizza? You stole his gal."

"I don't think so."

"I don't trust Scandinavians," Bledsoe said.

Dorn studied him to see if he was kidding, but couldn't tell.

Neither of them was aware that Dandy Cashing was the one most likely to first plant a load of buckshot where Dorn's suspenders crossed. However, Dorn mentally added him to Bledsoe's list of his newfound friends who would bear watching.

And Dorn also realized that if Dilly knew about him and his turtledove, he'd have the whole army after him.

"Well," Dorn allowed. "I guess it's glory enough for one summer."

"I reckon," Bledsoe agreed. "Why don't you just haul ass?"

"Bat Dorn doesn't run."

"Bullshit." Bledsoe said.

That had a familiar ring to it Dorn thought, as though someone had made the same response before to the same remark.

The following morning at "supper," Dorn acquainted the Phoebe with the apparent dimension of their problem.

"You'll have to be careful," she cautioned. "Why not pull out?"

He almost said, "Bat Dorn doesn't run," but was afraid to risk her reply.

After he left she was deep in thought for a long while. She had no intention of losing him again.

CHAPTER 21

GENERAL Tom Rounder, president of the Sioux Falls, Yankton and Fort Littleworth Railroad, was as unique in his own way as his construction foreman, Big Harry O'Phender. For one thing he weighed as much as Big Harry O'Phender, but the thing that made it noticeable was that Rounder was about a foot shorter. Consequently he looked something like a football. He, like General Lacey, had been a bright ornament in the Confederate pantheon of hard-drinking generals—a cavalryman, like Clay Beauford. In fact during the war Rounder and Romanza had been almost inseparable.

General Lacey had already been over to consult with Tom Rounder in the railroad company's offices at Sioux City, hoping to pave the road for a special plan he had in mind.

He'd told General Rounder, "Tom, you won't believe the change in old Clay Romanza. He acts tetched. Had an orderly like that once. I finally found out he'd been walkin' up a wagon tongue when he was a kid and slipped off and cracked his marbles on a whiffletree."

The two old comrades were sharing a big slug of Kentucky hundred proof and cigars in Rounder's office.

"How do you mean?" Rounder asked.

"Clay is plumb peaceful. As fur as I can find out he ain't shot anybody since the wah."

Rounder slammed his glass down. "No! Ah cain't believe it! Why, his honah got ruffled at least once a week. Hell, one stretch I had trouble gettin' a good night's sleep he kept me so busy deliverin' challenges."

General Lacey looked sad. "Yeah, I know. It's a plumb disgrace. I had to wait fer him to enter some flowers in a show before I could get him to come up here."

He had already acquainted General Rounder with the grievous nature of the stain on the family honor, so Rounder knew the pressing urgency of their current mission.

"Flowers?" Rounder snorted.

"Yeah. Hibiscus and azaleas."

"This is indeed a pathetic case," Rounder agreed. "How do you want me to help? I'll do everything in my power." He poured another snort.

"Well," General Lacey said, "the way Clay acts I ain't sure he'll go through with a duel with this Marshal Bat Dorn."

"Bat Dorn!" Rounder exclaimed. "I can see why even Clay Romanza might shy away from crossin' pistols with him."

"How come?" Lacey asked.

"Hell, even Wild Bill Hickok used to walk pretty keerful around Bat Dorn, the way I hear it. He kin fight with his fists, too. He kicked hell outa my foreman, Big Harry, and he's a moose—about half again as big as Dorn."

"You don't say? You reckon he might kill Clay in a fair fight?"

"Almost a dead certainty."

Lacey thought about that. "Then we'll have to do it fa'r 'n' squar', Texas-style."

"How's that?"

"Them Texans get 'em right whar the suspenders cross, they tell me."

"Clay won't fight that way," Rounder said. "I know."

Lacey laughed. "So what? We'll put somebody up in a barn or a tree or somewhere with a rifle. All we gotta do is get Clay to the duelin' ground. That takes care of my family honah, which is what counts."

"So what do you need from me?" Tom asked, but he didn't sound as earnest as he had earlier. He was getting a pretty fair idea of just who may have cracked his marbles on a whiffletree, and it wasn't Clay Romanza. Nonetheless, he could see no alternative now but to go through with his promise. Besides the honor of the Lost Cause was also at stake. That transcended purely personal consideration.

Before Lacey left, it was agreed between them that Big Harry O'Phender, who happened to be in town, and a few of his bhoys would escort Clay to Warbonnet to see that he didn't get lost, strayed, or stolen. . . . "Not exactly a prisoner y' understand," Lacey said to Tom.

"Right," Rounder agreed. "Not exactly. I'll tell Big Harry to choke him a little if he catches him wanderin' off. When you see Big Harry, you'll see how that might work real well." Then switching the subject, "Well, bring old Clay over. I've missed him."

When Romanza put in his appearance at the railroad office, the first thing he said to his good-living old football-shaped friend was "Tom! My, how you've grown."

They shook hands warmly. Tom Rounder was shocked to see that his old friend looked as trim and handsome as he had when the war ended. He was a trifle envious. Clay hadn't even lost any hair, although he did show some gray at the temples. "Christ!" Rounder said. "You must have found the fountain of youth."

"The next thing to it." Romanza was able to explain his situation to Tom, since General Lacey had left them alone.

All of this set Rounder to thinking. He admitted to himself that he would gladly have fought on the other side in the war if he hadn't been brought up on a diet of states right spiced with pellagra and prejudice. He had never eaten a square meal till he traveled north to work for the damn Yankees. Like Clay Romanza, he had been softened by affluence, and he felt a certain kinship with the dashing colonel. He would have hated to see old Clay die young in a damn-fool affair of honor.

"You know anything about this Bat Dorn?" Tom asked Clay.

"Nary a thing but what the general told me, and that's just his name. Apparently Breck is livin' in sin with him."

Tom grinned disarmingly. "And what have you been livin' in with Lorena Pulsifer-Jones?"

Clay laughed. "Luxury, for one thing, thanks to her."

"I don't want to tramp on your corns, Clay, but just why the hell did you let Breck get away?" Tom asked. "You could have gone after her."

"And have to work?" Clay blurted out.

"I see," Rounder said. He did, too. "Well, it looks to me like you're fair out of this. Why rush back in?"

"It wasn't my idea. It was Lacey's. He's plumb crazy about the disgraced family honor. Seems like so much hogwash to me."

"Then why go through with it?" Rounder said. "Bat Dorn can shoot the balls off a man at a hundred yards, they tell me. You'll get killed. He ain't gonna fight no stand-up duel either. Out here they start with the pistol in a scabbard. The fastest man and best shot wins. He's greased lightnin' on top o' bein' a dead shot. You'll need some o' them hibiscus and azaleas on an early grave if you ask me."

Rounder poured them another round. He eyed his old wartime buddy with deep concern.

Clay said, "I got a leetle confession to make. I wasn't exactly plannin' to shoot it out with anyone."

"What, then?"

"Lorena is out now makin' arrangements to see as how that crazy old goat Lacey disappears."

Tom's eyes darkened, "Permanently?"

Clay shrugged. "Lorena's got a good business head. I always leave details to her."

Tom lifted his glass in a salute.

"You came to the right town to hire a job like that."

After Clay had departed, Rounder pondered just exactly what instructions he'd finally give to Big Harry O'Phender. He was torn between his ingrained, lifelong honor and his loyalty to the sacred Lost Cause on one hand, and his friendship with Romanza on the other. An idea how to get out of his dilemma occurred to him. He sent a messenger to Lorena Pulsifer-Jones, unbeknownst to Clay.

* * *

After leaving the railroad office, General Lacey went over and telegraphed the Warbonnet *Clarion.* His message read: "To Bat Dorn and the Citizens of Warbonnet. Stop. Will be coming to town to satisfy the family honor. Stop. Will be on the historic first train into Warbonnet. Stop. P.S.: Signed: Clay Romanza."

The *Clarion* printed it all, including the P.S.:. It then editorially added "Clay Romanza killed twenty-one men in duels beore he was twenty-one, we are told. The general's train is scheduled to arrive on Friday at 12:01 P.M., and what follows should be mighty interesting. For those wanting tickets to go back East, the same train pulls back out at 9:00 P.M., following the big celebration. We understand that Big Harry O'Phender and some of his bhoys will be coming in on that train too. We wonder what Big Harry may have in mind. Squaring some old accounts? Look out, Bat Dorn!"

Below this was printed the comment of Bat Dorn obtained by the newspaper's reporter: "Bat Dorn doesn't run!" No editorial remark followed it, Dorn was happy to note when the paper came out. That was on Tuesday.

Dorn was reading the paper when Turk Bledsoe found him.

"I've located Big-Nosed George's camp," Turk said. "Or rather Pronto has. I'm headed out to get some help from General Dilly. You comin'?"

"You bet."

General Dilly placed a detail of cavalry under command of Major Pizza. He explained, "I'd like to come myself, but the whole thing is touchy. If they go after the major for doin' somethin' illegal, I want to be in the clear so I can defend him. And, he thought, if I'm unsuccessful at that it'll be his bad luck, not mine. To Dorn he said, "As U.S. deputy marshal, you're in charge of this affair. Major Pizza will take your orders."

There were twenty men in the detail, plus the major, Dorn, and Bledsoe. With Pronto as guide, they made a considerable cloud of dust as they headed for the mountains. Dorn figured Big-Nosed George might spot the dust cloud and get out of their way. He mentioned it to Major Pizza, thinking they had better move only at night.

Before he could convey that added thought, Pizza called Pronto over. He said, "You Injuns are on to all the tricks. How can we hold down this dust so our quarry won't spot it?"

Pronto studied the major solemnly for a moment, appearing to be turning that over in his mind. He finally said, "Plenty easy to do."

"How?" the major asked.

"Camp here," Pronto said.

The major looked disgusted. "Even I know that."

Pronto shrugged. "Then why ask Pronto?"

Dorn intervened. "That's what I was going to suggest anyhow, Major. No sense in scarin' Big-Nosed George away. We'll move at night."

At dark they resumed their approach on Big-Nosed George's hidden camp. In the back of Dorn's mind was always the need to return by 12:01 P.M. Friday when the train was due to arrive. He was growing fond of being Bat Dorn and recognized that he had a reputation to live up to.

They beat their way through gullies and over hills all night. It was growing light and they still had not reached their goal. Dorn noted Bledsoe and Pronto in consultation. He rode over to join them, Major Pizza following him.

"What's the problem?" the major asked.

"We're lost," Bledsoe confessed.

Pronto looked greatly offended. "We're not lost," he said. "Big-Nosed George's camp lost. We're right here."

Pizza shook his head, looking at Dorn for guidance. "We'll

camp here," Dorn said. "Pronto can scout around and see if he can find his bearings."

"I'll go with him," the Pinkerton agent stated.

Dorn watched them disappear over the bluffs. By evening they still hadn't returned. Meanwhile Dorn had got a good long snooze. He and the major were having coffee and a cigar.

"Where the hell do you suppose they are?" Pizza wondered.

Dorn had his suspicions in view of Pronto's record up till then and expressed them. "Lost," he said.

Pizza snorted. "You really think so?"

"Of course."

"That's rich," the major said. "A gawdam Injun lost twice." He looked at Dorn expectantly. "Waddaya wanna do now?"

"Go back to town. I gotta be there by Friday at 12:01."

"Let's see," Pizza said. "That's Friday the thirteenth. I hope you haven't got something big planned."

CHAPTER 22

DORN returned alone to Warbonnet on Thursday. The first thing that caught his eye was the unloading of several freight wagons at Sarge's new joint. The building sported a big freshly painted sign proclaiming it as Bat's Place.

I'll be damned, Dorn said to himself. He did name it Bat's Place, just like he said he would. A warm feeling for his pard overwhelmed him for a moment.

He saw Sarge busily supervising the unloading and dismounted at the hitch rail in front of the place. Sarge saw him coming. He swung his arm expansively around. "All ours," he proclaimed proudly.

"If I live long enough to run it," Dorn said.

"Hell, I wouldn't worry about that."

"I wouldn't either if I was you."

Sarge patted his shoulder encouragingly. "Cheer up. C'mon in and have yer first drink on the house."

The inside was as good as Sarge's brag that it would make the Bilgewater look like a dump by comparison. It was brilliantly lighted by cut-glass chandeliers. The bar was at least seventy-five feet long and already stocked with glasses and bottled goods.

"What'll it be?" Sarge asked, going around behind the gleaming polished mahogany bar.

"Make it a double double double. I need one."

"Of what?"

"Your best Kentucky bourbon, ya idjit. I haven't changed my brand."

"Hold on," Sarge said. "We can't have you hung over for the big openin' ceremony tomorrow. We're gonna cut the ribbon after the crowd of bigwigs blows in on that first train. They done druv that last spike while you was out sashayin' around the sagebrush. Which reminds me, Bledsoe blew in with Pronto and said if I was to see yuh, to say they got back okay. Where the hell was they?"

"Lost," Dorn said, meanwhile appreciatively eyeing the half tumbler of amber booze Sarge had poured for him.

Sarge said, "Injuns don't get lost."

"Pronto does. All the time."

Dorn tossed off his whiskey and reached for the bottle to pour another one. Sarge pulled it away. "Uh-uh. Save it till after the weddin' tomorra."

"Whose?" Dorn asked.

"Mine," Sarge told him.

"Who the hell'd marry you?" Dorn snorted.

"The widdy O'Neal."

"Marie?"

"You know any other widdy O'Neal?"

Dorn quickly grabbed the bottle, danced away from the bar, and poured another stiff hooker.

Sarge eyed him warily. "You mad 'cause I beat yer time with the widdy? I figgered you had the Phoebe 'n' them two Injuns."

Dorn thought, And that ain't all, podner. He was surprised, however, that he kinda liked the notion of Sarge and Marie. The two kids couldn't have a better pa than Sarge, nor one any better able to support them right. He might be a touch shy on moral indoctrination, but so what? Eating came first.

Dorn grinned and offered Sarge his hand. "Hell no, I ain't mad," he said. "Congratulations!" That, in fact, solved a dilemma he'd been thinking about. Now he wouldn't have to ask Marie to marry him so the kids would have a pa. He wondered if she'd have had him. Then another thought struck him. He asked Sarge, "Waddaya gonna do about whichever one o' my Injun wives yer married to just now?"

Sarge winked. "No problem," he assured Dorn. "I pensioned 'em both off, just in case. Five bucks a week as long as I can afford it. They like eatin' regular better'n anything. I reckon that'll leave you free to play house with the Phoebe, too, without worryin'."

"Thanks," he said, but he hadn't forgotten Clay Romanza—a real crack shot. Likely if Dorn was lucky enough to plug Clay first, he'd have to duel General Lacey next. In view of Lacey being Breck's father, Dorn knew he couldn't hurt the old man. Then there was Big Harry, very likely with a crew of his gandy dancers to back him, to say nothing of Yahoo Dave and his crowd. It figured to be a prime Friday the thirteenth for Dorn. Somehow he didn't seem to be as worried as he should have been. The bourbon had had that general effect on him. He was more concerned over Marie O'Neal's scandalous carryin' on with him when she'd probably known perfectly well that she'd marry Sarge if he popped the question.

"What're you thinkin' about so heavy?" Sarge asked.

"Women," Dorn said.

"So what's new?" Sarge asked. "I shoulda known. Oh, that reminds me, I got a perfumed envelope fer you." He handed it to him.

Dorn opened it and read: "I must see you as soon as you get back to town. Breck."

"Why not?" he thought. She had boilerplate under all the floors in her apartment, so at least he wasn't apt to get shot accidentally by some overenthusiastic celebrant puncturing the ceiling of the saloon downstairs with a .45 slug. He headed for the door.

Sarge said, "Somehow I figured you'd be leavin' after you read that note. Be sure to be back tomorrow morning at ten o'clock sharp."

"For what?"

"To deck yourself out in the new duds I got fer you to be head cardsharp around this joint. Also fer the weddin' at eleven."

"I'll be here. You didn't think I might skin out, did you?"

Sarge grinned. "Bat Dorn don't run," he said.

Bat turned and went outside. It was getting dark.

At the Bilgewater he spotted Pronto huddled in his usual snooping spot. "Ain't I seen you someplace?" Dorn asked snidely. He planted himself in front of him. "What happened to Big-Nosed George?"

"Heap haul ass."

Dorn turned and headed inside. He had almost asked the kid, How the hell would you know? but hadn't wanted to hurt Pronto's feelings. He thought, Hell, we all have our off days. He hoped he wasn't going to have one tomorrow, recalling that he didn't do too well on Friday the thirteenth as a usual thing, not that he was superstitious.

He found the Phoebe upstairs in her apartment. She slipped into his arms and kissed him fervently. She drew back and said, "Thank God, you got back. I thought maybe they'd already dry-gulched you."

"Who?" he asked.

She gave him a look. "Almost anyone. I wouldn't put it past Papa and Clay to sneak in ahead of time. Even Big Harry or Yahoo Dave might try to shoot you. And you just made it worse by running Fancy out of town. I could have handled him here. Now we don't know where he is and can't keep an eye on him. One of the bartenders told me he had a long talk with that martinet lieutenant right after you gave him his walking papers the other day. Fancy passed him some money. The lieutenant doesn't have something against you, too, does he?"

"Not that I know of." Dorn told the polite lie. He could hardly tell her the truth. She might laugh, but you never knew about women. She was more likely to try to fix him up to sing soprano, as Sarge would put it.

The Phoebe went on. "You've simply got to get out of town. At least for a while. I'll go with you." Somehow she didn't sound convincing. He suspected she knew he wouldn't run, and didn't want him to.

Again he caught himself about to say, "Bat Dorn doesn't run." Actually, however, the idea did sorta make good sense. But he knew he couldn't. Not now. He was in too deep, his reputation was at stake, and a lot of people were counting on him. A perverse notion nonetheless impelled him to tease the Phoebe a trifle. "Why not?" he said. "The sooner we run, the better. Start packing."

He was watching closely for her true reaction. She appeared startled. "You don't really mean it? Bat Dorn wouldn't run. Think of the Code of the West."

"To hell with the code," he said.

She looked disappointed. "You're kidding me, aren't you?" Her tone was almost pleading, though he suspected she'd go with him even if she thought he'd lost his nerve. He hadn't quite suspected that she was as proud of him as she appeared to be, even though she was the only one who knew who he really was; and she certainly knew he was not a well-known gunslinger from down South.

He sighed. "Of course I'm kidding. I wish I wasn't. But I can't run."

She looked a lot happier. There was still a lot of unreconstructed Southern belle in Breck. She'd rather see her man dead than "dishonahed." It was the moving spirit that had bled the South to death.

She said, "Let me pour us a nightcap, and then we'll go to bed."

"Not till I take a bath. I must smell like a goat, or at least like Pronto."

He contentedly sipped a bourbon, sunk into a tub of hot water while she rubbed his back, wearing only her "house coat," as she'd delicately referred to what she wasn't wearing in Pizza's picture. The part of her nearest him occasionally tickled his deltoids as she worked on his tired muscles. His troubles receded into the back of his mind for the moment. He thought, "I'll think about them tomorrow. At Bat's Place."

He had a surprisingly untroubled sleep after they finally

got to sleep. Breck snuggled close to him all night. They were by now so closely attuned to each other that they turned together as one whenever one or the other wished to turn over.

He came to life slowly in the morning, stretching and yawning. He opened his eyes to find the tomcat Cupid staring directly into them.

"Good morning, fathead," he greeted the cat and got a solemn blink for his pains. He rolled over and looked around for Breck. She was just rolling in the tea cart loaded with breakfast. He got up and surveyed the food hungrily. The cart overflowed with dishes of ham, bacon, sausage, eggs, rolls, butter, jam, coffee, cream, and even a decanter of cognac. His cigars were laid carefully beside his coffee cup. What a woman, he thought.

"Ah," he said, "the condemned enjoyed a hearty breakfast."

"Don't joke," she said.

He wondered if it would be a joke.

Down at the livery stable Dandy Cashing and Fancy Venere were just rolling out of their blankets in the hay mow. They'd sneaked into town well after midnight. Venere went over to the door through which the hay was loaded and peeked out through a knothole.

"Perfect," he announced. "You can see the whole street clear down to the depot." He patted his Winchester. "Now all we gotta do is wait." Dandy had a Winchester that was the twin of Fancy's, both furnished by the latter out of his own pocket.

"You ain't gonna chicken out are you, kid?" Fancy asked ominously, gripping his rifle suggestively, like a villain in a melodrama.

"Hell no!" Dandy said. "I owe that bastard Dorn plenty. Wake me up when the ball's ready to open and I'll give him a waltz." He rolled back into his blankets.

Venere looked at him calmly going back to sleep, and muttered, "By God, I believe him."

On the 12:01 train, General Lacey fidgeted nervously, frequently pulling out his turnip watch. "Couple of hours yet," he announced to Clay Romanza.

At the rear of the car Big Harry O'Phender was slumped in a seat, dozing. Several of his men were with him. Some more were at the opposite end. Big Harry had received his orders and fully intended to carry them out to the letter. General Rounder had told him, "After you see to your job for me, I don't give a damn if you tear Bat Dorn and Warbonnet apart. It wouldn't be good for business later on, but they'll write it off to the celebration that's natural on the day the first train hits town." General Rounder himself was riding in his private palace car. Several political dignitaries, scheduled to make long-winded speeches at Warbonnet, were riding in another special car. The general knew they would need their wind for something besides speeches if the donnybrook came off as he expected it to.

Similar thoughts occupied Yahoo Dave's mind. He'd pulled his men into town en masse. They were oiling up in the saloons, staying on remarkably good behavior. Cantoon was keeping an eye on things for his boss, who hadn't yet put in an appearance. Cantoon had developed a genuine fondness and respect for Dorn, as had most people in the town. He'd formed a plan to keep Dorn's skin unperforated, but wasn't sure how to carry it out. He knew that Bat wouldn't willingly skin out. Nonetheless, Cantoon was sure that if he could get the marshal out of town, most of the serous trouble wouldn't be apt to happen. Without Dorn, he figured there'd just be a routine killing or two, nothing serious, and for the rest, it would be busted skulls and a cutting or two.

When Dorn put in his appearance on the street it was

nearly time to go over to Bat's Place. He strolled down the street, outwardly calm and unhurried. The eyes of most of the population followed him. If there was anyone in town who wasn't aware of what was set to happen in Warbonnet this day, it had to be someone who had just blown in. Most of the folks from the hinterlands had come in to watch the fun, the homestead families having packed picnic baskets for the day. The tension in the air was so palpable that it almost crackled. Dorn nodded and spoke as he usually did to the people he met along the way, breaking the lawmen's code by smiling to quite a few of them, especially the ladies. He reached Bat's Place at ten sharp. Sarge was at the door to meet him.

"C'mon back in our offices," he invited. "Wait'll yuh see the furniture and doodads I got us." He led the way. At the rear were two offices side by side, with a hallway between. Both were deeply carpeted and furnished with walnut desks, leather swivel chairs, guest chairs, couches, and armoires. A decanter of Kentucky bourbon and glasses stood on sideboards. "Both exactly the same," Sarge said. "I didn't want to pull rank."

"Nice of you." Dorn smirked.

Sarge opened some boxes on his desk. "Our duds for the weddin'," he explained. "They're the same you'll wear as a cardsharp around here."

"You expectin' a lot of weddings here?"

"Only twixt damn fools and cyards," Sarge said.

"I'm probably the biggest damn fool you'll ever have in the place. I oughta head back down South where I'm famous, and where I'd have a better chance of stayin' alive. You got me in this Bat Dorn mess, come to think of it."

"Nemmine," Sarge said. "I told you not to worry. Leave it to me."

Dorn looked him over for some evidence of false confidence. He could see none. He must have a sound plan. Sarge was basically a practical and efficient manager—with a scheming mind to go with it. He was tempted to let Sarge do the worrying. However, he could recall one or two fiascos that had resulted from leaving it all to Sarge. His mind wasn't wholly on getting into his new outfit.

When they were both dressed, Sarge opened a closet door. There was a full-length mirror inside. "How about that?" Sarge asked, whistling at his reflection. Dorn forebore mentioning that his friend reminded him of a monkey in a zoo. He even had a stovepipe hat. But Dorn's own image was no more reassuring. He reflected that these togs might come in handy for his funeral. He tried to dismiss the thought, but couldn't quite manage. He checked to see if his guns showed too obviously.

He thought, I'll sure miss the Phoebe. But then, I won't know about it, most likely. He wasn't too long on believing in the hereafter, but it was a nice hope. If there was one, he'd always figured he'd go to the one with the good company and bum climate. On the other hand, he thought, the Phoebe will undoubtedly go straight to heaven. They'd like an angel that looks like her. He'd always been sure, since he was old enough to know his first one, that golden-hearted whores undoubtedly went to heaven—if there was a heaven.

"Well, best man," Sarge said, "here's your stovepipe hat." Dorn was surprised to see that Sarge's hand trembled a trifle. He felt a little shaky himself. Funny, weddings did that to men. It was worse than an impending battle.

Sarge said, "The preacher wasn't too long on doin' a weddin' in a saloon, but twenty bucks sweetened him up a lot."

They went out together. Doc Carruthers was there to give away the bride. Mattie and Hattie were decked out in white as bridesmaids and fitted the role well, their dusky skin contrasting attractively with the white gowns and caps. They both carried bouquets of prairie flowers.

"You got the ring?" Sarge asked Dorn nervously.

Dorn felt in his vest pocket, but his mind was on the 12:01, which was undoubtedly roaring westward at full throttle. He felt the ring right where he'd thought it was. "It's here," Dorn said. "Now, shut up. You're makin' me nervous, too."

He noticed five hard-looking hombres in the crowd, dressed in gamblers' frock coats. He nudged Sarge. "You know that bunch?" he asked, indicating them with a nod of his head.

"Yup. I hired 'em a while back by letter. I'll introduce you after the ceremony."

Dorn was puzzled. They didn't exactly look like gamblers, but he figured that's what they must be. He'd have preferred it if Sarge had left the hiring to him.

Marie O'Neal arrived, looking almost like a young girl. The ceremony was brief, attended by all the townspeople who could crowd into the building, which was almost all of them. Little Annie was a flower girl. Her brother Abe took it all in, wide-eyed, and got into the beer and ended up drunk.

Following the "I do's" the family friends crowded around the bride for their ceremonial kisses. When it was Dorn's turn, Marie held his head for a moment, then turned his ear to her lips. "Good-bye," she whispered. "It would have been you if you'd asked." There were tears in her eyes.

Dorn felt a lump in his throat and got away quick before he had tears in his own eyes. He'd always known what a tragedy it was that he couldn't marry all the women there were, or at least all the good-looking ones. His last words to her were "Sarge is a good man. Take care of him."

Right after the ceremony Sarge said to Dorn, "After we have some punch and cake I gotta see you back in the office."

Dorn's stomach didn't feel like it needed punch and cake. Breakfast hadn't been too bad, but that was earlier. He thought he knew now how a condemned man felt less than an hour away from the noose. He wondered what Sarge had in his scheming head. Before he found out, Cantoon approached him. He seemed a little embarrassed.

"Trouble?" Dorn asked.

"No more'n usual. That comes later. That's what I wanted to talk to you about. You gotta get the hell outa town till things blow over at least."

"No way," Dorn said.

Cantoon looked hurt. "You figure I can't handle the place alone?"

"I didn't say that."

"I got a buggy and fast team out back. No one'll blame you for leavin'. I even got a big trunk in the back. You can hide in that the first few miles so no one'll see you leave." Cantoon had, in fact, commandeered Persephone Dilly's trunk in which Dandy Cashing had been delivered to Wells Fargo a few days before. Everyone in town had, by then, heard of Dandy's recent misfortune, but none knew the entire story except Persephone and Dandy.

"So, you want me to pull a Dandy?"

"Why not?" Cantoon said reasonably.

"I'll think it over," Dorn said, seeing Sarge motion urgently to him. "Sarge needs me right now."

Cantoon tagged right along with him and entered Sarge's office. Inside were the five strangers Dorn had seen earlier. All were tall, lanky towheads with cold blue eyes, and all with a remarkable family resemblance to one another.

Sarge introduced them like a true master of ceremonies. "Bat," he said, "I done got yuh some replacements, since you'll be workin' here rather than marshaling after today. Meet the Hong boys."

Everyone in the West had heard of Warburton Hong—or Warby, as he was known—and his fighting brothers. Collectively they were known as the Fighting Hongs. They'd tamed plenty of western towns and made all the newspapers.

Warby Hong laid his cold, impassive blue eyes on Dorn. He shook hands with a strong, wiry grip.

"Glad to know yuh, Bat. We heard plenty about yuh."

Dorn grinned. "Down South?"

Warby looked blank. "Up here," he said. "These're my

brothers—Varney, Mart, Jeff, and Wild." They all shook hands with Dorn. Cantoon was watching, looking pleased. This could solve his problem about keeping Dorn's hide in one piece.

Sarge said, "If you'll hand over your badge to Warby, your problem'll be over. You can pull out for a while till things blow over, then come back and take over here. You need a vacation anyhow."

Bat pulled off his badge and handed it over. "These boys may solve my official problems. I reckon they could keep a lid on hell from what I've heard. But I've got a personal problem: Bat Dorn don't run. Remember?"

Cantoon had edged around behind him, anticipating such a reaction. He buffaloed Dorn as easy as he could with his pistol barrel applied to one side of his stovepipe hat. He said the appropriate "Bullshit!" under his breath regarding the Bat-Dorn-don't-run eyewash. Dorn collapsed slowly, and Sarge caught him before he hit the deck.

An hour later, when Dorn came to, he was in a dark confined space, being jolted roughly around. He could smell cedar shavings. He wondered where the hell he was and how he'd got there.

About a mile short of Warbonnet the 12:01 stopped briefly. Big Harry O'Phender escorted, or more accurately, forcibly hustled General Lacey to the door of the car. Waiting outside were Chief Snare Drum and a number of his braves. A short while earlier the chief had had a little confab with his old friend General Rounder.

Rounder had explained Lacey's problem to the chief. "See that he doesn't come back soon," Rounder had cautioned.

The chief pointed a thumb at his chest. "Leave him to me. He'll be gone for two snows," he promised.

"That's the ticket," Rounder said, passing a bunch of greenbacks to the chief.

The Indians took General Lacey away on a swaybacked

nag, cursing mightily all the way. As the Indians and their captive rode away from the train, a close observer would have noted that one of the chief's men looked a lot like the detective Turk Bledsoe, in an Indian disguise. Pinkerton's had done a lot of business with General Rounder before and had always delivered the goods, just as in this case. Bledsoe was a master of a thousand disguises.

The train pulled out, the engineer holding down the whistle to let Warbonnet know it was soon due in. Tension in the town mounted to a fever pitch when 12:01 passed with no sign of the train. It pulled in, finally, thirteen minutes late, on Friday the thirteenth, a historical fact of profound insignificance.

Big Harry and his crew poured into the town, waving pick handles. There were a hundred or more of them. At the same time, as though by prearrangement, Yahoo Dave's men, perhaps another hundred, streamed out of the saloons and joined the railroaders. The cry went up from them: "We want Dorn! Where is the bastard?" They marched in a detemined mass up the street, howling like demons. The street cleared of townsmen, who crouched behind closed doors, but peeked out windows to watch.

Warby Hong silently stepped into the road, his ominous intent emphasized by a double-barrel shotgun slung loosely in the crook of his right arm, two long-barreled pistols bulging under his somber, flapping black coat. The wide-brimmed black hat was pulled low over his grim face and burning blue eyes, which shone from under the brim like a pair of lanterns, even at midday. His brothers, similarly garbed and armed, filed in behind him, two on either side of Warby, looking equally grim and threatening. They set off silently down the middle of the road toward the approaching mob, small puffs of dust rising where their boots struck the road in perfect rhythm. They were actually in step like a military squad. It added still another ominous dimension to their silent progress.

Big Harry, striding a few steps in front of the mob, noticed them, stared for a moment intently, then halted in his tracks in surprise. He turned and held up his huge arms, bringing his followers to a milling halt. Voices from the rear shouted, "Git goin'! What the hell's holdin' up the parade?"

Big Harry shouted loud enough to be heard even above the mob noise: "It's no use, boys. That's Warby Hong and his brothers."

A grim, unhappy silence fell over the crowd. They'd all heard of the fearsome Fighting Hongs, and they recognized what this meant. A loud voice expressed it, growling, "Gawdammit, it's gittin' so a feller cain't join a mob anymore anywhere in the West without them killjoys showin' up to break it up 'n' spoil the fun."

Someone else said, "Let's git a drink 'n' fergit the hull thing."

"Yeah, let's," a chorus of voices chimed in.

The mob slowly dribbled away.

EPILOGUE

DORN had had considerable time to think things over while he was inside that trunk. He couldn't believe that his friends had abducted him, assuming that someone else had laid hands on him and by coincidence also employed a trunk to spirit him away and probably to do away with him. He was saddened by the knowledge that he'd left a pretty mess behind. Not at all like in books where all the loose ends got tied up. He hadn't found out, for example, who'd killed Square Deal O'Neal, though he'd bet it had been done at the orders of Fancy Venere. He hadn't captured Big-Nosed George. And he hadn't been able to catch General Dilly running with the rustlers, and he never would have, either, since it had been an even more improbable party with long blond hair who'd been the phantom rustler—the one that had written him perfumed notes—but Dorn would never find that out. On top of that he had no idea which of his enemies had abducted him. He couldn't make out at first, from inside the trunk, what the unusual noise was, growing in intensity and becoming alarmingly louder until it shook the ground. Then he realized it was the sound of a train approaching. He wondered if someone had placed him on a railroad track for a messy demise and braced himself for the crunch when it came. It never did. The noise stopped, but the steam kept puffing rhythmically like a breathing monster. Then he felt himself being hoisted aboard and carried somewhere, finally to be deposited on a solid surface. The train jerked into motion and he followed its acceleration by the rhythmic click of the wheels picking up speed.

In a while he heard the trunk being unlocked. He braced

himself to leap out and fight for his life. The first thing he saw astounded him. It was the Phoebe. Behind her he could make out the appointments of an elaborate and lavish drawing room. He thought perhaps he was losing his mind—or that perhaps he'd died and gone to heaven after all.

She smiled and said, "I hope you weren't too cramped."

He felt a sudden let-down. In fact, he was completely limp for a while. His head started to hurt like hell. He'd almost forgotten that due to his apprehension while he'd been in the trunk. A lump was a mild inconvenience compared to impending death.

"You're not mad at me?" she asked.

He forgot his condition and shook his head, then wished he hadn't. But he was alive; minor pains didn't count. Being alive was a lot more than he'd expected to be at this time.

"Where are we?" he asked.

"In General Rounder's private car. He was generous enough to let us use it. He's an old friend."

I'll bet, Dorn thought. A girl like the Phoebe probably had hundreds of "old friends" like General Rounder. Some men would have been jealous. But Dorn had had a good long time to think about what was really important in life while he'd been in that trunk expecting the rest of his life to be pretty short. It struck him as a fairly good world just the way it was. For some reason he turned and retrieved his plug hat, which had been under him in the trunk. He couldn't imagine why anyone had thrown that in with him. He poked the crown back into a rough semblance of its original shape and put it on.

"Where are we headed?" he asked, looking as ludicrous as he suspected he did. He grinned. He didn't care where they were going.

"Back to old Virginny," Breck said. "We can fix up the old plantation. From what I hear, it needs it. I have a notion my father won't be using it for a couple of years."

She'd had a talk with General Rounder and knew how it

was with father. She'd also heard about Clay Romanza. She couldn't believe he'd been reconstructed, but was happy with whatever had happened. She even thought of refunding the money that Lorena Pulsifer-Jones had paid to get rid of her father for a while. Then she remembered that the two of them had been screwing her out of her money for years.

Just at that moment, Clay Romanza and General Rounder, two old comrades in arms, were back at Bat's Place, helping with the housewarming.

The Phoebe didn't care where Clay Romanza was. She had sense enough to know that what she'd once felt for Clay had been infatuation with his wartime glamour and good looks.

Dorn was looking her over now with loving eyes. Her eyes met his and read the expression. She was still his youthful dream, no matter what the passing years had done to both of them.

"Would you like to get married?" he asked.

"As soon as I can get a divorce," she said. "I thought you'd never ask."

They came together in a long, close embrace, kissing tenderly.

Bat Dorn was headed back down South—where he'd been famous first. Warbonnet would never forget him. Grandfathers would someday tell wide-eyed grandkids about him. "Even Wild Bil was keerful around old Bat," they would say. "It took the five Hong boys to keep a lid on Warbonnet after he left. Why, I remember the night old Bat and me . . ."

And none of them, not even Sarge, ever knew his real name. That's the way it is sometimes—when legends are made.

Glenn G. Boyer was born in a log cabin in Wood County, Wisconsin. He spent twenty-two years in the U. S. Air Force and retired as a command pilot with the rank of lieutenant colonel. While an Aviation Cadet in Santa Ana, California, Boyer met members of the Earp family and went on to become the doyen of historians of Wyatt Earp and his brothers, amassing a vast research collection that became the basis for numerous publications. Among the most notable of these have been *The Suppressed Murder Of Wyatt Earp* (1967), concerned with the development of the Wyatt Earp mythology, publication of the memoirs of Josephine Earp as *I Married Wyatt Earp* (1976) that also served as the basis for a motion picture for television, and more recently *Wyatt Earps Tombstone Vendetta* (1993). He is currently at work on a definitive book collecting his numerous articles and essays about the Earps, Doc Holliday, and other historical personalities involved in the Earps years in Arizona. With *The Guns Of Morgette* (1982) Boyer launched a second career as a novelist of the American West. In his series about the adventures of Dolf Morgette and together with the novel, *Dorn* (1986), he readily established himself as one of the finest authors of the Western story, with fiction as notable for its sharp and penetrating characters and grippingly suspenseful plots as for the authenticity and accuracy of the historical backgrounds and settings. His next Five Star Western will be *Morgette And The Shadow Bomber*.